NIGHT OF THE
WITCH-HUNTER

PATRICK BARB

NIGHT OF THE
WITCH-HUNTER

KILLER VHS SERIES
BOOK 6

SHORTWAVE
PUBLISHING

Cover illustration by Marc Vuletich.
Cover and Interior design by Alan Lastufka.

First Edition published March 2025.

10 9 8 7 6 5 4 3 2 1

ISBN 978-1-959565-64-2 (Paperback)
ISBN 978-1-959565-65-9 (eBook)

This is a story about witches. The ones who came before and the ones waiting to make their presence known.

CHAPTER ONE

When the classroom VCR quit working halfway through her presentation in U.S. History, Josey knew she was in trouble. Gears spun faster and faster inside the machine's dusty black casing. The high-pitched squeal made everyone, including her teacher Ms. Roberts, cover their ears. It was worse for Josey, standing at the front inhaling chalk dust fumes, helpless beside the monolithic, black TV/VCR media cart rolled in on presentation days for students (like Josey) too shy to stand with poster board or diorama and read from note cards, shaking with nerves.

She was close enough to hear the out-of-control VCR gears devouring the magnetic tape from inside her cassette—destroying her recorded project. Desperate to do something, anything, she smashed her fingertip against the EJECT button. Pressing it over and over, sometimes with a fast jab and, other times, holding the button longer to see if it made a difference.

It didn't.

Goddesses, help me.

Nikki was the reason she'd started using phrases like that. Nikki was the one always going on about earth goddesses and Tarot and witches and other impossibly cool things whenever they snuck into the woods behind school, smoking menthols stolen from Nikki's mom, complaining about teachers and their snobby, ultra-judgy classmates at Fallen Church High. Josey wasn't sure how much of the actual magic component she believed. But, then again, pleading her case to a goddess certainly seemed more viable than praying to God—that one from the Bible with the beard and the smiting of sinners and Jesus too.

As if intervention, divine or otherwise, had seen fit to come to her aid at last, the VCR belched out her VHS, sounding like a dying robot in a sci-fi flick. The black cassette, hot to the touch, emerged first. Then, the ruined magnetic tape spilled onto the pilling, tangle-weaved carpet.

Watching from her podium, Ms. Roberts wrung her hands and folded them one over another, mumbling prayers.

And it was all going so well before this! A detached, sardonic tone to her thoughts came easy to Josey. However, there was truth to her words. She'd worked hard on the project. The assignment? Cover an aspect of their town's history and demonstrate how it tied into a broader national history topic.

She'd picked the witch trials. Or, in the case of Fallen Church's past, the *singular* witch trial.

* * *

Josey had taken a shoebox full of scribbled-on, spiky-haired Barbie dolls from a neighborhood yard sale and "dyed" one of the doll's hair black through an intense permanent marker scribble session. One her mother had watched closely to ensure no stray marks ended up on her precious kitchen table. That doll was Josey's star, set apart from the other dollfolk which she'd kept blonde or auburn-haired, paired with shorter-in-stature He-Man, G.I. Joe, and Power Ranger figures borrowed from the homes of kids her Mom had her babysit—their parents only agreeing to take on Josey's services because of her family's standing in Fallen Church.

Then, she'd used her Nan's sewing machine and patterns she'd downloaded from a historically accurate doll clothing message board to create period-accurate, 1600s New England garb sized for her "cast." It was extra, different, unexpected. It was exactly the sort of thing Josey loved to do.

Her fingertips displayed the scabs and scrapes from the sewing needle whose tip ended up rust-colored when all was said and done. Josey imagined the dolls and action figures also had enough of her blood in and on them that her enemies could use the toys as voodoo dolls—if they bothered to go that far.

Her raven-haired, plastic-molded featured player "stood" on a makeshift display base of cardboard, her stiff arms rising and falling in jerky stop-motion, surrounded by other dolls in coarse black woolen jackets and dresses.

Josey's monotone voice-over demonstrated how she was the one person in her family who'd mastered all the video editing and recording equipment her dad purchased years before to film Christmas morning present-opening sessions, but had never quite got around to using. Syncing the audio and visuals wasn't exactly easy. So, there were moments when Josey's recorded voice lagged behind the on-screen visuals.

* * *

JOSEY: The town of Fallen Church, New Hampshire isn't as well-known as our New England cousin, Salem in Mass-achusetts. But we share a common historical bond. The bond of American witchcraft.

While those accused, tried, and executed in Salem numbered around thirty, our hamlet saw just one resi-dent charged with "consorting with the Devil, spoiling the innocence of village youths, and tempting elders with her wanton lust and debauchery." All of that's real too. You can read it for yourself in the town records.

* * *

Josey had added a quick cut to a new shot at a wobbly angle, the best she could manage in the one-room town archives located downtown in a small, non-descript brick building adjacent to the town hall. She'd had one long drawer of museum-quality artifacts pulled open for viewing, her camera zooming in and out until she focused on a crinkled yellowed piece of parchment that'd served as a broadside displaying the news across the New Hampshire colony and was now preserved under a slab of glass. This official notice served as Josey's proof and evidence that she understood primary sources—one of the particular requirements of the assignment.

But when the document appeared on-screen, her classmates paid little to no attention, certainly not enough to give any signs of being impressed by her discovery.

* * *

JOSEY: Rebecca Josephine Wesley, who'd lost both her elderly parents on the sea voyage from England to the Colonies and who'd finally settled alone in the village of Fallen Church in the New Hampshire Colony was formally accused of witchcraft in 1693. At the time, the Puritans controlled almost all aspects of life in the New England Colonies. Following a trial during which Rebecca was blamed for nearly every misfortune affecting the township and which she was not even present to testify on her own behalf, she was sentenced to die.

However, initial execution plans did not live up to expectations. The "witch" survived attempted drowning and hanging. Even getting crushed between boulders could not end the young woman's life. Indeed, according to the records at least, her body was revealed to be remarkably unscathed after the top stone slab was rolled away. It was not until she was set ablaze, burned at the stake down to ashes and bone, that she finally expired.

* * *

The next part of Josey's overly ambitious production involved a gasoline-soaked doll and flickering flames, melting globs of plastic sizzling on the asphalt of her family's driveway. It was the highlight of the whole endeavor as far as Josey was concerned. The recording even caught her tiny, whispered "Yes," uttered as she peered through the viewfinder.

* * *

JOSEY: Rebecca was survived by a son,
newly-born at the time of her capture.
A bastard, with no father's name
provided in the village records.
William took his deceased mother's last
name. The Wesley line continued in
Fallen Church as a result, with male
heirs born in each subsequent generation. Until me.

Today, I am the first and only blood-
related female descendant of the Fallen
Church Witch Rebecca Josephine Wesley.
Part of my name—Josephine 'Josey'
Wilhelmina Wesley comes from hers. I
am. . .

* * *

Josey had turned from the TV cart and faced the rows
of desks before her, all occupied by her bored and
bemused classmates. She held out hands filled with
the crinkly remnants of her video tape.

She willed herself to try and find the words to
extract herself from this disaster, the ones that'd allow
her to sit down with some dignity intact, returning to
her seat at the rear of the class where she'd pull her
too-large black leather jacket off her seatback, drape it

over her head, and sleep—her participation grade be damned.

Unfortunately, she wasn't quick enough for Ashton Gore, he of the All-American curly blonde hair, pristine white home game football jersey, and too-shiny smile obscuring his often more sinister intentions. He banged both thick pink fists on his desktop and chanted—low at first, but letting the volume rise with each strike: "witch, witch, witch, witch, witch. . ."

In the classroom, the other members of the football team, their hangers-on, and those kids who saw which way the wind was blowing and didn't dare risk association with Josey by abstention, all picked up the chant.

"WITCH! WITCH! WITCH! WITCH!"

Even as Josey rolled her eyes, attempting to appear unaffected by the taunts, tears blurred her vision. Their presence made her desk seem suddenly much farther away.

Suddenly, a hand gripped her upper arm, squeezing it tight.

Keeping a hold of Josey, Ms. Roberts's nostrils flared and her bottom lip quivered.

"Young lady," she said, each syllable followed by a hitched breath, a theatrical performance of outrage, "remove this blasphemous videotape from my classroom immediately. Take it to the dumpster behind the gymnasium, put it there with all the trash."

An outraged voice inside Josey whispered retorts:

My ancestor didn't do anything wrong.

I didn't do anything wrong either.

Did you even watch my tape? Did you listen to the words in the report?

These witches—here, in Salem, all over—were never the villains. The people who accused them, who testified against them, who took them from their homes, their families, and ended their lives, they were the bad ones. They were the corrupt, immoral ones. They used people like Rebecca as scapegoats.

But instead of speaking up, Josey let silence fall across the classroom. Ashton and his hangers-on smelled blood in the water. Putting a fist over his mouth, he faked a cough, "covering" a too-loud "Witch! Bitch!"

The outburst set off a new rolling tide of laughter.

Screw this! Josey thought.

Stopping at her desk to pick up her jacket, but leaving her books and backpack behind, she stomped in scuffed Doc Martens to the doorway and made her exit, pulling the door closed after her. But not slamming it.

The tape came too.

CHAPTER TWO

Nikki stood by the dumpster, cigarette smoke curling past her fingers, obscuring the emerald polish she'd applied to her nails that morning. Josey couldn't remember the last time she'd felt so happy to see another person; but she was certain that whenever that time was, the person she'd been grateful to see had to have been Nikki then as well.

Nikki, with her long, straight naturally auburn hair. Nikki, wearing a thrift store-purchased Army jacket over a long-sleeved purple top and a brown skirt that fell to her ankles. Nikki, displaying her Goth bona fides in black combat boots, heels thick and unashamed, and by a pile of charm necklaces draped around her neck, displaying ankhs, inverted crosses, and pentagrams, a veritable bouquet of occult symbology.

Cigarette to her lips, she sucked in smoke. At the same time, she fished in her satchel for a pack of smokes, flicking the box top open and offering it to Josey.

Saying nothing yet about what'd brought her to the dumpster, Josey reached into her best friend's bag and retrieved one long, thin menthol. She held it to her mouth, while Nikki made a quick one-handed search inside the satchel for a lighter. "Presentation went that well, huh?" she asked, breaking the silence first.

Something between a sob and a laugh exploded from Josey. Finally, the tears came. For real, this time. She knew she wouldn't have to hide them from Nikki.

Her friend plopped onto the concrete in front of the dumpster, keeping a soft hand around Josey's wrist. She didn't squeeze tight or pull down, but made space for Josey, let her know it was there—if she wanted it.

Soon, Josey rested her head on Nikki's shoulder. She studied a dark brown mole under Nikki's chin. A single aberration in an otherwise perfectly pristine snowfield of pale skin. To Josey's thinking, that solitary blemish made the other girl appear that much prettier. She hadn't told Nikki that, though.

The red-head girl ran her fingers through Josey's hair, the green-painted nails becoming jewels in the darkness of the brushed-aside strands. They stayed like that for a while. Outcast girls before the dumpster.

It wasn't long enough as far as Josey was concerned.

* * *

"Roberts called the video *blasphemous*?" Nikki asked with a throaty chuckle, after blowing another smoke ring.

The mint smell of their menthols undercut the stench of school garbage, but didn't eliminate it entirely. Josey had smoked a single cigarette and scraped the cherry off on the bottom of her shoes before flicking the butt into the dumpster. One was more than enough for her.

"Yeah, she did," Josey said. "She sucks. This school sucks. This town sucks. This whole. . . this everything. . . it—"

"Hey now!" Nikki cut off Josey's rant, a wry smile appearing on her face. "It's gonna be the new millennium soon. Everything's gonna be different like those posters downtown say. Or ya know, maybe the world's gonna end. Or something."

Her lips thinned, her expression turning grave and serious.

That lasted until she blew another smoke ring, and the devious smile from before crept back onto her face.

"You *bitch*," Josey said with a matching grin. She playfully shoved her friend's shoulder.

"So, wait. Was the Fallen Church Witch *really* your great-great-great-great-however-many-greats grandma? Like for *real*?" Nikki asked, changing conversational direction with manic ease.

Ever since meeting Nikki in middle school, when the new girl's family moved to town, and she'd finally, *finally* felt like she'd found someone who truly got her and everything she was about and wanted to be, Josey had learned to embrace her friend's chaos.

"Yeah," she answered. "You missed out on the fifth-grade class trip to the execution site. They used to do a reenactment on the anniversary of her execution. Or at least they did until *that* year. . ."

Nikki's eyebrow raised. "What happened?"

Josey shrugged.

"I started crying when the woman—probably just an acting student, college girl taking a semester off from Juilliard or the like—was playing the part of Rebecca, burning at the stake.

"It was weird. We were standing in the place where this woman was killed, but it was so clean, those period-authentic cobblestones reeking of ammonia. Then, it melted away and I had, like, a vision of how it was back in the 1600s. I mean, what it must've felt like. When I looked at the girl playing the part of my ancestor, her face was different. More like my face. But not quite, you know? Close though.

"And the skin, her skin, my skin—all of it was on fire. I saw roaring flames shoot up in twin towers of orange, red, and yellow. I was screaming by that point. Next thing I remember, my teacher's pulling me away from the reenactment. Dragging me.

"Then, I dunno, I wasn't there with the class anymore, so I'm not sure what actually happened. I didn't see it, but I heard secondhand what happened. The girl playing Rebecca started screaming and it *wasn't* part of the show. She screamed and collapsed to the ground. Then, everyone got quiet. That silence lasted until someone finally went to check on her. Lot of kids who were there that day claim that they rolled this girl over and. . . her face was red. Like a bad-*bad* burn. Skin all blistered."

"No freakin' way," Nikki said. "All this time we've been friends and you never mentioned this? Not once? Dude, you've been holding out on me, Joe."

Josey knew the other girl well enough to detect notes of offense beneath her friend's playful tone. She shrugged again. "It's not something I like to talk about. It was pretty scary."

Nikki flicked her still-lit cigarette away from the dumpster and it bounced off the brick exterior of their school building. Its neon orange cherry struck the gray mortar, resulting in an all-too-brief miniature fireworks display. Then, she wheeled around, grabbing both of Josey's wrists and pulling her friend upright, surprisingly strong for how slight she appeared.

"You know what we gotta do, right?" she asked.

Josey's eyebrow arched. "What?"

"We gotta have a séance. Let's get you in touch with your witchy ancestor. Get the real story from the source. How cool would that be?"

Josey pulled her hands free. "I dunno. . ." she said. "I mean all that occult stuff you like, it's just. . ."

"It's in your blood, remember?" Nikki asked, smiling in a way that Josey had found she couldn't possibly say no to.

Inside the school, the bell rang for the next

period. Josey's shoulders slumped as she realized that she'd have to slink back to Ms. Roberts's class for her stuff.

On the bright side, at least her next class was Art with her and Nikki's favorite teacher, Mr. Mundy. Hippy-dippy Mr. Mundy liked the so-called "weird" kids, and, as a result, would never mark them tardy.

"Oh, c'mon Joey," Nikki said, again pulling out a nickname that she and she alone was allowed to use, "let's get ole Great-whatever Grandma Becks chatting, maybe we convince her to freak out some of the prudes in this godforsaken town. Maybe she'll even give Ashton a poltergeist wedgie."

That last bit earned her a smile from Josey. Once she saw it, Nikki pressed her advantage. "Come onnnnnn, we'll do it tonight. What were you gonna do on a Friday night anyways? Go to the game? You, me, the spirit of your ancestor, we'll make it a girl's night. What do you say?"

"I think. . . I think. . . Okay, fine, let's do it," Josey said, relenting

She stared at the ruined video cassette in her hands, realizing that she hadn't thrown it away yet. Hadn't wanted to. *Didn't want to.*

"What am I supposed to do with this?" she asked.

Nikki was already at the door, ready to re-enter the swirling chaos of Fallen Church High's mid-class change. She shrugged this time.

"I dunno," she said. "Give it to Mundy. Maybe he'll use it for one of his big multimedia collage art installment thingamabobs. His exhibit's gotta be ready soon, right?"

The door opened from inside the school. Mr. Hoskins, the school's janitor with his dripping Jheri curl cascading down to rest above the blue, starched collar of his uniform shirt stared at the girls.

"Ladies, get ya asses inside," he said. "I swear, y'all trifling at this school."

The duo ran past him and into the building, laughing, cackling. Josey still held onto the ruined tape.

When the door closed behind them, she stopped short for a moment, glancing over her shoulder, back the way they'd come.

A strange feeling passed through her. Strange, but *not* unfamiliar. Like cold fingers on the back of her neck or a half-remembered whisper from the end of a dream.

CHAPTER THREE

The girls sketched occult sigils, symbols with so-called mystical power that they'd either found on the web or copied from heavy metal CD covers, in chalk onto black construction paper during art class. The witchier and more demonic-looking the better. Making his rounds to inspect each student's project for the day, Mr. Mundy —his close-cropped salt-and-pepper beard, short hair, and cardigan hiding a hippie past that revealed itself in the far-away look in his eyes—hadn't objected to the girls' choice of subject matter. Instead, when he'd seen what Nikki and Josey were working on, he'd laughed.

"Far out," he said. "Must be the season of the witch, huh?" Then, he'd shuffled along to the next student. The white drop cloths hung around the room hiding Mr. Mundy's own work-in-progress art exhibit from prying eyes, wavered as he passed on by.

His words about the "season of the witch" remained fresh in Josey's mind hours later, as Nikki—

leaning against her friend's dresser for support and making herself as long and lanky as she could—finished her impression of Mundy's burn-out drawl. "I love him," Josey said, batting her eyelashes playfully.

Having Scotch-taped the final sigil they'd drawn in class to the window at the rear of Josey's bedroom, Nikki flopped onto her friend's fluffy bed. Her ear grazed the curve of Josey's tight-black-jeans-clad leg. "Who? Mundy?" she asked. "Didn't take him for your type. . ."

Josey, feeling more than a slight tingle from the closeness of Nikki's cheek to her thigh, scooched away an inch or two, moving toward the pillows. ("Leaving some room for the Lord," as her brother's church group leaders might say.) "Yeah. I mean, like, I respect him. He's super cool. Certainly much cooler than a lotta folks in this town. Sucks he never got outta here, but I guess it's good for you and me. . ."

As she let her answer trail off, a woman's voice echoed up to the girls from downstairs. "Josephine, sweetheart! Your father, brother, and I are heading to the game, okay?"

Her mom's heavy Boston accent stretched the "sweetheart" and "father" to a "sweethAHRt" and "fahhhh-thaaaa."

The girls giggled. Then, Josey cupped her hands around her mouth and shouted, loud enough to be heard through her closed door. "No, Ma! We're good."

"Alright, you girls have fun with your little art

(*aHt*) project or whatever," her mom replied. "C'mon Tommy, Sean, let's get this show on the road."

Josey's little brother Sean was a freshman and he was in the marching band. That, plus the church group, where he volunteered at the seniors' home and at an after-school kids' program at the YMCA, meant he was the family's goodie two-shoes, always making Josey look bad in comparison. On the bright side, however, Sean's extracurriculars were great for getting their mom and dad out of the house, leaving Josey all alone.

If it weren't for Sean and his marching band commitments, she and Nikki wouldn't get the chance to try out the spell that would maybe, possibly, allow Josey to speak with her witchy ancestor. Nikki had dug it up from some website she'd found killing time on one of the school library's computers, waiting for her sister to pick her up. "Everyone on the message boards says it's legit," Nikki said, "And you *know* you can trust the word of internet nerds."

When they heard the side door downstairs close and the garage door rising, Nikki sat up. The creaks and moans of the old faux colonial house were as close to silence as they were likely to come.

"Alright," Nikki said, "First things first, run down and get some salt from the kitchen for the summoning circle. I'm gonna start lighting some of these Dollar Store candles."

* * *

Soon, the only light in Josey's bedroom came from some twenty to thirty candles Nikki had brought over. Sitting atop the carpeted floor, each flickering flame undulated within glass containers of varying sizes. Thin wisps of smoke curled to the ceiling from blackened wicks. An almost overwhelming intermingling of scents followed—everything from vanilla to watermelon to "sea breeze" and a gag-gift scent of dog turd. It reminded Josey of shoving a bunch of different gum flavors in her mouth all at once on a dare and chewing, chewing, chewing. She hoped she'd get used to it— and not barf like she had with the gum.

Josey offered to reimburse Nikki for the candles. But Nikki would have none of it.

"C'mon, get serious," she said, "how many times am I gonna get the chance—are *we* gonna have the chance—to talk to someone from the past? Someone who might be a *witch*? This one's on me."

Josey let it go. She was pleased to have a friend willing to go to such extremes to make her feel better. She thought back to reading *The Handmaid's Tale* the year before in English class. She and Nikki had devoured it like no other book before.

What was it the main lady in the book said or wrote or whatever? Something in Latin...

Oh yeah. Don't let the bastards wear you down.

As far as Josey could tell, Fallen Church was chockful of bastards. Had been for a long, long time. Maybe forever. That was something she'd have to ask her ancestor about. She unfolded the printout Nikki had given her. Her friend had even taken the time to highlight Josey's parts, making certain she wouldn't miss a word.

Sitting cross-legged on the other side of the salt circle from Josey, Nikki breathed in deeply. Then, exhaled. Her pale cheeks had an amber glow to match the red of her hair. "Ready to do this?" she asked.

"Ready as I'll ever be. . ."

"Close your eyes. . ."

"But how am I supposed to rea—"

"Not forever, dude. Just for now. For my part."

When Nikki laughed, it didn't hurt. When Nikki laughed, Josey wanted to join in and she did. As their chuckling tapered off, Josey began to feel the proverbial weight of the near darkness surrounding them and the supernatural implications for what they were about to attempt, regardless if it worked or not.

Nikki started to read.

"Ancient spirits. Goddesses. I call upon Circe, Hecate, the Horae. Sisters all, I sing your song. Open the door. . . just as we open our eyes to you."

Taking that as her cue, Josey's lids rose. She brought her page close to her face.

"Don't!"

Josey shook her head. She thought for a moment that she'd heard someone crying out from far away. A young woman. But on a Friday night with a football game, that sort of cry could've come from anywhere. She guessed it was one of their classmates, someone much *cooler* than her or Nikki. At least as far as the Fallen Church High ecosystem was concerned.

"*Don't!*"

Again. This time, it sounded more like a warning. Closer too. She peered across the candlelight at Nikki. The other girl hadn't moved, didn't look like she'd heard that voice crying out in the night.

Josey chose to read on. She figured it was just her overactive imagination causing her to think she heard things that weren't really said. She didn't want to back out, though. Didn't want to disappoint Nikki. That was absolutely the last thing she wanted to do.

The ritual had to continue.

CHAPTER FOUR

Fallen Church, New Hampshire Colony, in the Year of their Lord 1693...

"Goody Rebecca, show yourself, vile woman!"

The witch-hunter's voice boomed louder than the downpour that soaked the leaf-strewn ground cover in the woods surrounding the village. His cries rose above the booming thunder and crackling lightning strikes. The tall, brittle branches splintered and flash fires crackled, only to be extinguished by the ever-present deluge.

Goodwife Rebecca, her dress and undergarments drenched equally by rainfall and the blood she'd shed bearing a child scant hours before the hunter's pursuit, shivered in her hiding place—a shoddy lean-to constructed in a frantic scramble. She'd leaned long-dead branches against the low-hanging limb of an old oak. The coverage they provided was minimal. Fierce winds blew rain back into her face, forcing her to push soggy strands of her raven-colored hair away from her eyes over and over again.

Still, it's better than nothing, she thought.

Running barefoot from her home after the witch-hunter was spotted by the lone midwife willing to aid an already shunned young woman, Rebecca's soles were shredded, more of her blood spilling onto the forest floor. The scent of blood mingled with that of wet leaves, wet everything.

A new noise—an explosion—interrupted her thoughts, stopping her private beseeching to the entities she sought for their protection and guidance.

Lightning. . . she thought.

But that notion left her head with the sudden splintering of the branch above her. Wood chunks fell upon her. The sulfurous stench of gunpowder made its foul presence known.

Panicking, Rebecca saw his figure silhouetted by the rainfall. The witch-hunter. The one who'd vowed to the Fallen Church elders that he alone could bring her to heel, that he alone would make her pay.

Goodman Nathaniel Pryce. A scholar. A gentleman. A witch-hunter, or so he advertised his services.

On hands and knees, she scrambled from her now-exposed hiding place, searching in downpour-heavy darkness for escape, salvation. Strangely, as she moved, the darkness, the rainfall, both seemed to recede in equal measure.

Tiny fires appeared, encased in glass and dotting their surroundings. A mad blend of scents mundane and exotic filled Rebecca's nostrils, even as the odors of wet leaves and blood diminished. Only the noxious gunpowder odor remained as strong as before. Its combination with the new, inexplicable scents was enough to make the young woman gag.

Her eyes watered. Clearing her throat, she saw her nemesis with blunderbuss raised. Gun smoke swirled from the end of its barrel. His dark, water-logged, wool-spun clothing sloshed as he moved, soaked through so Rebecca could watch whole droplets descend from his coat. The tiny flickering lights shining from the ground exposed this so-called witch-hunter with his features tall and wide on a pale, bloated face. Round pupils like black discs, nostrils flared, lips stretched to reveal crooked yellowing teeth.

"Come out, abomination. Come and prepare to receive the Lord's vengeance."

Kneeling on the water-logged ground, Rebecca ached all over. The pain went beyond physical, venturing into mental, emotional, and spiritual planes.

She'd heard rumors, gotten wind of whispers and innuendo, and noticed pointed fingers from the corners of her vision. People spoke of Salem, of the witch trials there. But they'd gone silent, looked the other way, as if to pretend there was nothing for anyone to fear, nothing to worry about whenever Goody Rebecca came near.

And yet, she'd *known*. She'd felt it in her bones

along with the kicks of her boy-child as he grew fat and plump in her belly.

"These will o' wisp lights are a clever trick, girl. Unfortunately, they only serve to make your position clearer. My hunt will end soon, and your suffering will commence. . ."

"Oh my God, is that. . . is that her?"

This new voice sounded from somewhere impossible. It belonged to a girl, a young woman, something so familiar in her inflection and tone. Goodwife Rebecca brought chilled, damp fingers to her lips to make certain the words weren't issued from within.

"Concentrate, Josey."

Another voice. Another girl.

Pryce swung the barrel of his blunderbuss in sweeping arcs, clearly having heard the strange voice as well. He seemed to have no more idea who was speaking than did his prey.

"Who goes there?" he shouted. Gun in one hand, he used his other to reach for the cutlass strapped to his side.

"I thought this was a séance spell. I thought we were talking to a ghost. This looks like. . . what is this. . . ? These people. . . they're alive. *When* is this?"

"Good questions, girl," Rebecca muttered.

"Keep going. Keep reading," the other girl said.

An image flashed in Rebecca's mind's eye, overlapping with her known reality. A circle. Composed of white particulate, like grains of sand on the beaches where the colony ships had landed years before, spitting out an orphaned girl into a new world. But it wasn't sand.

Salt. They've made a salt circle.

It's a summoning circle.

But who are they summoning?

Her mind raced, drawing forth half-remembered rituals. She envisioned symbols whose creation she'd been instructed on during her dreams. As the memories grew clearer, her legs felt as if they were aflame. Ignoring the pain, she sprang to her feet when she heard those impossible girls calling her name.

"We invoke thee, Rebecca Wesley. Come to us, Rebecca. Come to us. Come to..."

Despite that sudden burst of energy, standing proved too much for the exhausted, bleeding young woman. She stumbled before the circle of salt and tiny fires.

"Come..."

Dead leaves and other forest debris stuck to her face, Rebecca looked into the wicked eyes of the approaching witch-hunter. Pryce tilted his head, like a feral cat preparing to toy with fresh prey. He pointed with his curved silver blade. But not *to* Rebecca. A new, unexplainable quarry drew the hunter's attention.

He pointed to the flames, to the circle, to the emerging visages of two young women—half there and half not—with each girl dressed in clothing unlike anything seen before in the Fallen Church of 1693.

Pryce walked with long strides, his every step filled

with purpose. Too weak to rise and stop him, Rebecca cried out a warning. "Don't!"

That word traveled forward, across a long forever.

Don't, don't, don't, don't...

Goodman Pryce, the witch-hunter, stepped into the salt circle and the tiny flames surrounding him rocketed to the treetops. Shining so bright that Rebecca had no choice but to close her eyes. And then...

He was gone.

Fresh tears ran hot from Rebecca's eyes. The rain was truly gone. Under a clear sky, she looked to the stars and made a wish, praying for the safety of the girls she'd witnessed.

They wanted me, she thought. *They wanted me to come, but now it's Pryce they'll have instead. Spirits, protect them.*

Then, knowing the Spirits might not provide enough protection, she dug her fingers into the wet earth below the layer of leaves and made preparations for a different type of worship. She could only hope that her magic would be strong enough.

CHAPTER FIVE

The Pilgrim lay sprawled on the carpet inside the salt circle Josey and Nikki had sprinkled around the floor moments earlier. He looked just like a reenactor who'd lost his way from Plymouth. Lying face down, his arms were thrown forward, hands holding a curved sword and a wide-barreled musket—*or whatever the gun's called*. His tall black hat tilted from his head and wet-ringleted, stringy black hair fell against the limp white shirt collar above his coal-black coat.

Whoever he was, wherever he'd come from, the man was thoroughly soaked. Pressed against the floor, dingy rainwater sluiced off his clothing. He emanated a potent musk, reminiscent of pine scent and stale body odor.

"Josey! The circle!"

Nikki's cry drew the other girl's attention to the rivulets streaming from the man and winding their way toward the salt circle. Knowing enough about witchcraft and summoning rituals from movies and

TV to understand that breaking the circle would be a *very* bad thing, Josey panicked and lunged forward. From the other side of the circle, she heard Nikki asking, "What are you doing?"

But Josey couldn't say for sure. She acted on instinct, letting the potent mix of adrenaline and momentum carry her along. Even with the salt circle near flush to the carpet, she raised her leg when stepping over the white granulated line, as if straddling a fence.

Stepping down into the circle, close enough to watch the black-coated man's back rising and falling with slow, steady breaths, Josey hesitated, allowing panic to regain a foothold.

"I don't. . ."

Her legs felt weak. That feeling—that sense of losing power—reminded her of the woman they'd glimpsed through flickering candlelight moments earlier. That woman's face was streaked with dirt and grime and forest debris, but remained familiar somehow.

Josey stumbled, as if a power greater than herself pulled her downward. She crashed to the floor. Reaching a hand out to slow her descent, her bare palm squelched against the wet woolen coat of the stranger.

The mystery man rolled onto his back with a quickness. Taking Josey—and Nikki as well—by surprise. Josey slipped back onto her ass, as the man, already on his knees, thrust his curved blade to stop just shy of her neck. The blade's sharp tip came close enough to nick her skin ever-so-slightly, drawing a trickle of blood that slid down the front of her shirt.

Josey recoiled, not only from the touch of the blade and the hot sensation of her blood brought outside when it was meant to remain inside her body, but also from the foul, wide-set features and the monstrous appearance of the strange man who attacked her.

"Where?" His voice emerged choked, gravelly.

"Where? Where? *WHERE?*" he repeated the query over and over, eyes flashing with intense madness. Black pupils round as dinner plates bulged, as their respective fleshy orbs pressed against too-small sockets.

Josey took a chance and scooted further away. However, in her frenzied escape, she didn't pay attention to where she was going or where her hands were placed. A single hand slid back to the circle, smearing the salt. Breaking it open.

All Josey wanted was to get away. Soon, the edge of a palm tapped against the heated glass of one of the summoning candles. The container tipped onto its side. A tiny flame danced from the wick and spread to the carpet.

A hand fell on Josey's shoulder, someone pulling her out of the broken circle and away from the fire already spreading across the carpet and leaping onto her bed. More than anything else, she was happy for the distance created between herself and the strange man who'd appeared out of nowhere.

No, not nowhere, Josephine. You know where—when —he came from. You heard who he called for. You just don't want to admit it.

Because that's crazy. It's... it's impossible.

Her rescuer, Nikki, crouched beside Josey. Maybe a little too close, as it sounded like she was yelling in her friend's ear and had been for a while.

"...out of here! C'mon!"

Josey rose to her feet, moving slowly, as if swimming up from the deep, dark bottom of a fetid pool. Her eyes remained transfixed on the flames skittering across the carpet. They enveloped her bed, then crawled up the walls to devour her Bauhaus and Type O Negative posters—Peter Steele soon consumed by the flickering tongues. Then, something rose before Josey, drawing her vision to a point ahead, a teeny dot becoming a widening circle. The man in Puritan clothing aimed his musket, the barrel lined up even to Josey's face.

Next, a *click*.

Then... a deafening *BOOM*.

Someone's—Nikki's, *of course*—hands grabbed Josey's hair, pulling her to the floor. Chunks of drywall and plaster rained down on the girls through the flames. Touched by fire, Josey's skin ached worse than the worst sunburn she'd ever felt. But it beat the alternative, getting her head blown off her shoulders by the musket ball that slammed into the wall behind her.

Desperate to get her bearings, Josey glanced around and found the man ranting amid the spreading flames, shaking his sword at the girls. While she saw his mouth moving, she couldn't hear a word, as her ears still rang from the recent weapon's discharge. Practically deafened, she turned to her friend. Both girls turned toward Josey's closed bedroom door. Their closest means of escape.

That was all the discussion they required.

Both girls crouch-crawled to the door. Once there, Nikki sprang to her feet, pulling her shirt bottom over her hand to act as cover. She twisted the knob fast and yanked open the door faster than that. She stumbled out into the upstairs hallway with Josey right behind her.

Risking a glimpse back, Josey caught the Puritan raising his musket once again.

As though sensing her eyes on him, he pulled the barrel aside for a split second. Long enough to smile at his prey, his black eyes narrowing, yellowed teeth jutting past fishy lips. Looking like a monster from Hell.

Then, Nikki grabbed Josey's wrist and pulled her from the doorway. The loud report of the musket fired again served notice to the girls—what they'd encountered inside Josey's room was *very* real. And very threatening.

He has to reload, Josey thought.

Moving on auto-pilot, she grabbed the doorknob on the hallway side. The hot metal against her bare skin made her cry out. But she bit her lip and pulled the door shut, hoping there was still enough time before the man had his gun reloaded.

"Josey, what are you doing?" Nikki asked.

Josey used her free hand to point to a heavy wooden console table resting against the wall outside her room. "Help me!" she yelled. "Move that here, across the door."

Nikki nodded and got to work fast. There was no hesitation. Only action. Once the table crossed the plane of the frame, Josey released the knob, leaving behind stringy bits of her blistered flesh. She grabbed the table as well, pulling while Nikki pushed until they'd wedged a corner of the tabletop under the already rattling knob.

"Let's go!"

This time, Nikki's words brooked no resistance. With her burned hand held like a shriveled crone's claw to her chest, Josey followed her friend in a panicked rush down the stairs. Passing family photos, amusement park caricatures, and other mementoes lining the walls. Behind the girls, the fire made its first tentative steps outside the bedroom and across the upper floor of the home. Josey's room, all her clothes, her CDs, her stuffed animals she hid at the back of her closet, everything inside her room was already gone.

CHAPTER SIX

The windowpane glass shattered out from Josey's second-floor bedroom. Shards of the broken pane rained down on the bushes bordering the Wesley's front porch. Moments later, with his heavy black coat waving behind him, the fabric singed along the bottom edge, the stranger from another time leapt into the night. He crossed his thick arms across his face, as though trying to protect his already awful visage from the worst of the fire and the broken glass.

Pressed flat against the foundation of her house, hoping the bushes which they dove behind when they'd made it outside would keep them out of the man's sight, Josey held a hand across her mouth, biting the tender, burned skin of her palm, trying her best to repress a scream.

The leaping man's momentum sent him over the porch, resulting in landing feet first onto the thin, dying grass of the front yard. One heavy-booted foot sunk into a pile of wet leaves and the other caught the edge of the concrete walkway.

The boot in the leaves slipped forward and the man's other foot, jarred by the impact on concrete, twisted to the side at a sharp, unnatural angle. The crack and pop reminded Josey of tiny gunpowder poppers tossed on the street by kids on the Fourth of July.

The subsequent *snap* of a twisted—quite possibly broken—ankle was seconded in intensity by the stranger's enraged howl that followed. Collapsing to the ground, his drenched clothes stained by grass, mud, and leaves, the Puritan pounded a gloved fist against the gray concrete. This rash act only increased his pain and rage in equal measure, as the walkway proved an unforgiving surface.

Nikki crawled forward, pushing aside branches as if she were about to make a break for it. Josey reached out and grabbed for her friend. When Nikki turned to face her, Josey put a finger to her lips, then held the finger up, signaling that they should wait.

Fire ravaged the building behind them and the strange man howled in pain just ahead. The girls found themselves in quite the unenviable position.

At least I know how to handle a fire. It's easy enough to run away, get help, let the professionals handle the rest.

But that man, though. . . if he's who I think he is. But no. . .

Curiosity kept Josey's attention on the man in black. She watched, transfixed, as he waved his hands slowly over his snapped and twisted, seemingly useless leg. It should've been impossible to hear anything over the roar of the fire, but Josey grew certain she *could* hear words mumbled from the injured stranger's lips.

His words weren't from any language she'd ever heard before. The words, ancient, alien, and forbidden, came to Josey a moment past when they must've been uttered. As though reality warped and shifted around the man's words, rearranging itself so that Josey would understand.

Like a video tape played backward, minus the squiggle of black, white, and gray static over the top, the stranger's leg turned itself back around the correct way. This change was followed by the sucking sound of bone pulled into its proper place. Finally, the flames leaped from his coat and the pebbles of glass scarring his visage popped out of wounds that would soon be less than memories in mere seconds.

Pop, pop, pop, pop.

Dusting himself off, the man turned to gaze at the shattered bedroom window through which he'd escaped. He held tight to his ancient weaponry, admiring the fire as it raged through both floors of the house.

"Pity," he said, as if he knew the girls were close enough to hear him. "'Tis a good fire for burning a witch. Or *two.*"

With a turn and flourish of his cape, its black cloth spread across the smoky gray sky, the stranger left the house to burn and marched down Josey's street. He moved as if he had no cares in the world or regard for the vast differences between the world of 1999 in which he'd emerged and the Fallen Church of many, many years past.

* * *

Crawling out of the bushes, their hair tangled, their eyes bloodshot with tears that cut across the gray-black greasy soot on their cheeks, Josey and Nikki moved like reanimated corpses. Reaching the edge of her lawn, where dying grass kissed the sidewalk, Josey rose on unsteady feet, grateful to be alive and free from the inferno she'd formerly called home.

Nikki stood beside her. Both girls hidden in shadows, stark and black, like silhouettes made of black construction paper. The house's burning exterior crumbled inward behind them.

The sharp sudden sucking sound, like bathtub water down the drain, was all too much for Josey.

Across the street, Mrs. Slayton, one of her uptight church-going neighbors, appeared as a pair of narrowed eyes peeking out between the parted slats of her vinyl blinds.

"It'll take a bit for the firetrucks to get here," Josey said, speaking as if she were in a dream and not just experiencing a waking nightmare.

"Huh?" Nikki's reply was concise and got her point across.

"Everyone's at the game," Josey explained.

"I assure you, lass, this is no game. No hoop and stick or Blind Man's Bluff. This is a witch hunt and you've got the worst of the witch-hunters on your trail now. Goodman Pryce won't stop until he's purified this town, remade it in his image."

The words echoing inside Josey's head, had come from the witch—the young woman Josey spotted during the summoning. The one they were supposed to contact. Not only did Josey hear the words in her head, but the witch appeared as a semi-translucent apparition in the teenager's mind's eye, manifesting from the twirling gray smoke spilling from the burning house and the crumpled remnants of the front door.

This vision of Rebecca Wesley had eyes that glowed neon blue like the hottest part of a flame.

Josey swallowed back a scream, letting it shrink to a whimper hidden by the rolling cry of a siren coming to life in the distance.

CHAPTER SEVEN

Josey couldn't say which was worse: her mother's crying or her father's loud lecturing with his overly dramatic gesticulating as a bonus. Even as the Fallen Church firefighters rolled up their hoses and broke up the last of the smoldering ashes formerly known as "home" with their axes, Josey spied her mom standing at the edge of their front yard and bursting into fresh tears. As she watched this, her dad positioned himself in front of Josey and launched into her with another variation of his "What were you thinking? How could you let this happen? Don't you care about your home? Don't you care about your family?" speech.

Josey had tried to explain what happened. Of course. They were her parents. They were supposed to believe her. It's why she'd chosen to stay even as Nikki had begged her to leave.

Now, perhaps Josey had left out some of the more supernatural details of what transpired from her account, but she'd at least cobbled together a narrative that included the strange man, dressed like the old Puritans, breaking into the house and threatening two teenage girls. Not only threatening but actively trying to harm them. He'd even gone so far as to fire a gun at them. *Twice.*

Unfortunately, the fire chief and police officers on-scene informed the Wesleys that the fire damage would likely cover up any corroborating evidence that might put the truth—*or* the lie—to Josey's story.

Frustrated to find her parents spiraling, reacting from a shock and disbelief rather than love and trust, Josey turned away from them both. Doing so, she spotted her little brother Sean watching the scene from across the street, still clad in his marching band uniform. He held his black plastic instrument case low, like he was some sad-sack cliché of a door-to-door salesman. His face gave away nothing emotionally. It displayed none of their mother's sadness or father's anger.

Coughing from the after effects of smoke inhalation and flexing her wounded hand under heavy layers of EMT-provided gauze, Josey walked over to her brother.

"Everybody's gonna be pissed at you," Sean said, avoiding his sister's eyes and focusing on the circus of departing fire trucks and police cars, alongside their neighborhood lookie-loos and busybodies—plus folks who'd driven by "just to take a look" or to "check up on things."

"What do you mean?" Josey asked.

"We won tonight's game. Not like *you* care. But, still, we won. But instead of getting to celebrate, everyone's gotta worry about what happened to our house. What *allegedly* happened in our house. . . And it's all because of you. And your little girlfriend."

Josey's mouth opened and closed, her mind racing a mile a minute to find the correct combination of words to convince her brother of the truthfulness (*in part*) of the tale she'd shared.

A sudden, freezing chill penetrated the jacket Josey had borrowed from a neighbor and her black and singed T-shirt beneath that, to access her bare skin. Whispered words followed in her head, from a voice that wasn't her own.

"The witch-hunter is close. Nathaniel Pryce will be here soon. This chaos is perfect for him, girl. He'll use it to his advantage. I should know. . . it's how he first singled me out, turned my fellow villagers against me."

Hearing those words, knowing who they were spoken by, Josey did an abrupt about-face and shouted to her parents, "I'm sleeping over at Nikki's!"

Her best friend was by her side in no time. Nikki had been fielding additional questions from Fallen Church P.D. Or perhaps it was better to say she'd been evading questions from them. Ever since her family moved to town with a few outstanding warrants from across state lines, Nikki's kin was far from friendly with the boys and gals in blue and black.

Now, side-by-side, the friends headed straight for Nikki's beat-up VW bug.

As if shaken free from their shock by their daughter's announced departure, Josey's mom and dad also beelined for Nikki's car.

"Whoa, whoa, whoa, whoa, whoa!" Josey's dad said, snapping his fingers and furrowing his brow, living the "angry father of a teenage daughter" cliché.

Her mom took a more subtle approach, holding her hands out, pleading with tear-filled eyes. "Josephine, please. Stay here with us."

Nikki, already in the driver's seat without having to be asked by her friend, turned the key in the ignition. The VW roared and then sputtered to life, drawing more eyes from the assembled masses near the burned-down house.

Josey stood on the other side of her friend's car. The passenger door was open but she appeared to hesitate. Her mother, perhaps seeing an opening, again attempted to convince Josey to stay.

"You should be with your family now," she said.

With those words uttered, Josey shivered again, the unnatural presence of her ancestor witch making herself known once again.

Ducking into Nikki's bug and settling against the cool faux leather of the seat, Josey called back to her mom, "That's just it, though. Believe it or not, I *am* with family."

She pulled the door shut. With the doors closed and the windows up, she cut short the squawk of a nearby police radio announcement. A dispatcher's voice was halted while sharing something about a "suspect in black. Appears armed. Maybe? Armed with wha—"

Josey pulled the seatbelt over her chest and clicked it into place. "Let's get outta here," she said.

Her father slammed his palms against the curved front hood of the bug. Already shaken by earlier events, both girls jumped out of their seats at the impact. His hands pressing down on the car, Mr. Wesley launched into a rage-rant targeting driver and passenger alike.

"Goddammit. Get the hell out of your freak friend's car, Josephine."

But even as her dad ranted, Josey was tuned into another voice, the witch still whispering to her descendant. Each breathless syllable felt like ice crystals in her ear canal before traveling to her brain.

"We must flee from this spot," Josey said, her word choice strange, her tone and affect flattened. After all, they were not her words, but those of the other.

None of her friend's out-of-character actions appeared to matter much to Nikki. She took her hands off the steering wheel, but only long enough to flip Josey's dad a double-bird middle-fingered salute.

Her defiant gesture set the middle-aged man off again and also got him to lift his hands from the car, balling them into fists.

What's he gonna do? Josey thought. *Punch the car?* The thought made Josey's pulse race. Her father had never been violent. Never hit or hurt her. But she had no desire to risk her safety or that of her friend.

Whatever Mr. Wesley intended, it came too little, too late. Nikki put the car in drive and pressed her foot to the gas pedal. She held the brake down simultaneously, making her tires spin. Josey's father leaped back, a stumbling ogre surprised by its prey's lack of fear.

And then, the girls were gone.

CHAPTER EIGHT

J osey stared at her ancestor's ghost hidden in the reflection of her eyes inside Nikki's passenger-side sun visor mirror. This spirit—or whatever it was—tilted its impossibly small head, studying her descendant across the ages.

Between the blue-green tint of the woman in dirty Puritan garb and the way her form was incomplete, marked by gaps all over like an image from a printer with low ink levels, calling the Rebecca Wesley before her a "ghost" was an easy enough decision for Josey to make. It was certainly more in line with what Josey had expected when they'd first undertaken the summoning ritual.

"Wait a minute. *Whose* ghost is inside you?" Nikki asked.

Ignoring the fast food and pharmacy bags strewn across her friend's ride, Josey remained focused on the apparition, the young woman in her homespun dress, whose pale, haunted face was streaked with what appeared to be mud. Grass and leaves decorated spectral tendrils of tangled raven-black hair.

"It's the. . . the. . ." Josey found it hard to even say the words.

"The witch, Girl," the apparition answered via Josey's voice, apparently having none of the same problems as her descendant.

"What, Joey? Why did your voice change just then?" Nikki asked, not taking any bullshit.

Joey would expect nothing less from her friend.

She swallowed and talked for herself this time. "My ancestor. She's *here.* Rebecca Wesley. Well, she's kind of here. It's like she's a ghost, except—"

"Ghost?!? I assure you, goodwife, I am no spirit from beyond the grave. Though, perhaps I am out of my time."

Josey covered her eyes, as if that might silence the new voice inside her head. "It's Rebecca," she repeated. "She's here. But not entirely. Not like. . ."

Nikki glanced from the road for a moment, trying to study her friend's face.

"I don't see anything. Or anyone," she said.

"Who is this?" Rebecca Wesley asked, speaking through her descendant.

"She's in there, I swear," Josey said with a shiver, her jaw aching from speaking double her normal amount.

"Ah," the witch said, *"you're of my line, eh?"*

Josey imagined herself nodding, hoping that might best convey her message to her ancestor.

Ahead of the car, a brightly lit neon sign rose from a parking lot, serving as a beacon for the girls and their not-a-ghost. For many Fallen Church's residents, there was nothing along the old highway access roads worth visiting. Junk lots; rusting, abandoned industrial and construction equipment yards; cheap storage facilities for those looking to store things that might raise eyebrows and for those hoping to store these things without supplying substantial information about themselves: this collective made the area a No Man's Land, populated by the dead and dying vestigial appendages of Fallen Church. Everything out that way was dead or dying, with the exception of that neon pink beating heart of a sign. It marked a spot just past Fallen Church's city limits. Atop a black metallic pole, one could find a several-feet-tall re-creation of an old Puritan church with steeple and cross inverted, appearing salacious and cattily sacrilegious, glowing against the night sky, beneath that an advertising message in black plastic: CHEAP BUDS / 2 FOR 1 LAP DANCES.

"Hey, hey," Nikki said, driving with purpose through the parking lot outside the neon-advertised adult-entertainment establishment, "I believe you, okay? I mean, after what we saw at your house. . ."

On one hand, Josey was relieved to have her friend trusting what she'd shared; however, her good feeling was marred by the realization that where her friend had driven them was very much *not* Nikki's house.

What strange lights are yonder? Be that a sign of the

Christian God? The Rebecca apparition asked inside Josey's head.

"No." Josey spoke, trying to head off any controversy.

"No what?" Nikki asked.

"No it's *not* a sign of a Christian God—"

Then, she added, "Dammit, Nik, I thought we were gonna go to your house."

Nikki had not brought them to her house. Instead, she'd driven them to "The Meeting Hall," Fallen Church's unassumingly named (and *only*) strip club. From the outside, the one-story brick building appeared like it must have during Colonial times. Sun-bleached, inclement-weather-battered bricks added a dusty, faded quality to the exterior. The modern lighting, spotlights set in the parking lot to shine back on the building, plus the tinted glass at the entrance beneath a covered walkway, served as the outside's sole nods to modernity. A frantic mix of pulsing techno and teased-up hair metal leaked out from inside the building, the sound loud enough to be heard even inside an old, beat-to-shit station wagon.

Nikki bypassed the rows of patrons' vehicles waiting in the front lot. Some of the nicer trucks and sports cars were familiar sights from their high school's parking lot. Josey supposed the football team was out celebrating their earlier victory. She had no desire to add a run-in with Ashton Gore and his neanderthals to the evening's growing list of bad experiences.

Not noticing, or maybe choosing to ignore, the way her friend tensed in the passenger seat, Nikki rolled the Bug, slow and steady, past the front door, slowing and honking her horn once, then twice, until she drew the attention of a beefy, muscular bouncer whose bald head and furrowed brow gave him the appearance of a wrinkled thumb. The man's practiced scowl fell away quickly upon noticing Nikki behind the wheel. He snapped out a quick, friendly wave.

Nikki rolled down her window and shouted, "Hey Maurice, how's business tonight?"

Maurice the bouncer shrugged. "Eh, we got some of the post-game crowd whose blatantly fake IDs I'm supposed to look the other way on. I tell ya girls, those little boys better play nice with my ladies if they know what's good for 'em, you feel me?"

"My sister working?" Nikki asked him.

Maurice nodded. "Yeah, DiDi went up earlier. Now she's back in the dressing room playing den mother to the other gals, I'm sure."

"Cool, cool," Nikki said. "Gonna go in through the back way then."

"You remember the secret knock?" Maurice asked her.

Nikki gave a thumbs-up and resumed driving, swinging the Bug around the building to its far less visited backside.

"*Ah, a house of sin and ill-repute,*" Rebecca said, no judgment detectable in her intonation as she spoke through Josey again.

"Thank you, ma'am. . . or Goodwife Rebecca, right?" Nikki said, catching on as to which member of the Wesley family was speaking at the moment.

For her part, Josey seethed as Nikki parked at an awkward angle, half-in and half-out of the parking space's faded lines close to the Meeting Hall's rear entrance.

"What?" Nikki asked, putting the Bug in Park and giving her friend her full, undivided attention.

"A strip club? Really?" In the past few hours, Josey had done magic, been shot at, and had her house burned to the ground. Her patience was wearing thin, even for Nikki.

"It's better here. Better than my house. Home's a mess. In more ways than one," Nikki replied.

Josey wanted to keep arguing, wished a witty retort and a dismantling of her friend's claims would both magically appear in her mind's eye. But nothing was coming to her.

Rebecca had no such problem.

"Does your neophyte recommend this den as a possible sanctuary?" Rebecca asked via Josey.

"That's her again. Isn't it? Wonder why she's not here like. . . like that Pilgrim Dude?" Nikki seemed all set to burst apart if she tried to hold her questions back much longer.

The magic is not strong enough inside this Ni-Key. That time, Rebecca's words were inside Josey's head, meant for her alone.

"What?" Josey asked out loud.

"What *What?*" Nikki asked right back.

"*You, Josephine...*"

"Josey," the witch's descendant said, correcting the apparition living in her head.

"*Josey, you. . . are tapped into powers ancient and primal. Forces beyond the mortal ken. A power created by entities flourishing inside the Earth itself. We share this power and therefore a connection drew my spirit to yours. I sensed your ritual on a strand stretched across the loom of time and snatched hold before it retracted to this moment, this far-flung future time for me, and what I suspect is your mundane present. But it was incomplete spell work, and as a result, I'm afraid I can only project my astral being into your body. My earthly form remains in my time, stuck in this moment before what I am certain is to be, or was, my end. Or the beginning of my end at least.*"

The witch's answer came with such a matter-of-fact tone, as if to put an end to further questioning from either girl—host or witness.

Josey stayed in the passenger seat of the parked car, overwhelmed by the information relayed to *and through* her. Her seatbelt was locked in place. Something more was needed to get her moving. Closing her eyes, she saw her ancestor's astral form floating before her. A spectral hand reached across the ages, connecting one Wesley woman to the next.

Oh, sweet child, Rebecca said, Let me add my powers to your burgeoning supply. If you like, I will teach you the ways of the witch."

Tired, frightened, and confused, Josey whispered, "Yes."

Reopening her eyes, Josey found Nikki's previously hinted-at fear and confusion making themselves more obvious. She held her black-painted lips slightly apart and her eyes shimmered. Even with another presence in her consciousness, Josey couldn't suppress a thought regarding her friend's beauty, even in this shared moment of vulnerability.

Ethereal, angelic, dark, and brooding, like a Romantic poet.

Again, she heard her own voice but the words uttered came from another.

"Ah, she loves you," Rebecca said, speaking through Josey. *"Then, that is why we will do as you say and enter what I imagine is a quite different Meeting Hall from the one I have known...."*

CHAPTER NINE

"Wait, *who* loves me?" Nikki asked, the arch of her penciled-in eyebrow suddenly growing more pronounced.

Embarrassed by her ancestor's declaration, Josey pictured herself swept out to sea, swimming desperately against the riptides. "Nothing," she lied, "it's nothing. It's the witch. She's inside me. Somehow. Magic, I guess."

Nikki nodded her head slowly. "O... kaaaay."

Then, "How am I supposed to know when it's *you* talking or when it's *her?*"

Josey placed her hands on her hips, cocked her head to the side, an incredulous expression on her face.

"Shall I perhaps whistle or mayhaps provide a hand signal by which you shall better recognize me?" That was Rebecca speaking, of course.

"Never mind," Nikki said. "Hi, Missus, uh Miss, umm Josey's family witch. We've all got a bunch of questions for you about what the hell's going on here, but my gas tank's running low and I gotta have enough to get home later and if we sit out here without the car on I'm pretty sure we're gonna freeze our asses off eventually. . . so, uh, can we go inside first?"

"Yes," Josey said. "Let's go."

Inside her head, the witch's voice told her: *"You're already improving with the use of your powers. But you'll need them all, especially if Pryce is on the hunt."*

* * *

After the girls knocked at the rear entrance to the club, Nikki's older sister DiDi opened the door with a face that looked ready for a fight. "What the *fu*. . . *oh.* NikNik?"

Her hair in bouncing, bountiful curls, turquoise eyeshadow and hot pink lipstick on her face, a silk robe cinched not-too-tight, DiDi's resemblance to her younger sister was there, hidden beneath a layer of sensual theatricality.

Nikki shoved past her big sister and went right into the club's dressing room. Josey scurried to keep up with her friend. As she did, the ancestral-projected spirit of her witch ancestor continued whispering about spells and demons and Godheads, like the secret song discovered on a new CD.

"Hey, DiDi," Josey mumbled.

"Hey Josey-Bear," DiDi said, before returning her focus to her sister. "Hey, hey, where do you think you're going?"

DiDi followed her sister with a dancer's grace, navigating a labyrinth of duffles and knock-off Donna Karan handbags, each one carrying changes of clothes or college textbooks or drugs and so many one-dollar bills, either wrinkled, rolled, crumbled, or crushed.

The women, *the exotic dancers*, were in various stages of undress, visible down a long stretch of folding tables that doubled as makeup stands. Mirrors, bordered by white-hot bulbs buzzing in their frames, were balanced two per table. In a corner of the galley-shaped dressing room, a dancer with curly black hair and a tattoo of a rose on her chest pulled red Lycra boots over long dark legs. A punky-looking Asian girl with spiky green hair and a nose ring sashayed over and helped the other dancer get the last inch or so of her thigh-high boot into place.

The scents of vanilla, jasmine, and sweat were in the air. The subtle flow of air conditioning from a vent near the ceiling brought forward goose pimples on everyone's exposed skin.

None of the dancers were particularly shocked or surprised by the presence of high schoolers in their midst. After all, Nikki's sister had worked at the club for a while. Long enough for Josey's parents to forbid her from hanging out with Nikki because of her sister's work and then forgetting about this ultimatum, their daughter's social life not setting off alarm bells for them.

In addition to the chill bumps, the exposed body parts glimmered with a fine glittery coating. Makeup compacts opened and closed, while clasps and straps for lingerie were snapped into place. Josey was greeted with quick nods and wry smiles. One woman, smelling tropical as she rubbed coconut oil on her legs, with hair as lush, luxurious and full-bodied as the rest of her, pointed to an empty canvas-backed makeup chair. Josey smiled at the woman and took her seat.

I know what this place is. Abandoning her running commentary on harnessing inner power and trans- muting outer magic, Rebecca addressed her descen- dant directly.

"What is it?" Josey asked, too exhausted by. . . everything, to give a damn about anyone noticing that she was talking out loud to what would appear to be no one at all.

This is a sisterhood. A coven. You'll find sanctuary here. Safety. I envy y—

From another corner of the dressing room, DiDi's voice rose sharply. "You burnt down *what???* And you came *here???*"

Nikki attempted to shush her sister following this outburst. Unlike the girl's arrival, DiDi's words drew focus to the interlopers. Suddenly, Josey didn't feel quite as safe as her ancestor had assumed they'd be.

A knock echoed from the other door to the dressing room, the one on the opposite end that the dancers took to access the club floor. Its jarring interruption startled Josey.

Taking control of the situation, DiDi leaned away from her sister, cupped a hand to her mouth, and shouted at the door, "Dammit, Murray, I know for a fact that Candylynn's set ain't over yet and we got Misty, Christy, and Xenia in the VIP, everybody else back here, our breaks are still going, so. . ."

She trailed off as if she expected an answer, but silence greeted them from the other side.

Finally, a man with a gruff South Boston accent answered. "Uh, ladies, you don't by any chance got some, girls. . . Look, I got a fella here, says he wants some bit. . . huh? Are you serious? Yeah, alright, whatever you say, pal. This fella here tells me y'all are harboring witches?"

The chuckling of the man on the other side of the door was cut short when another voice was heard, indistinct but sounding low and rumbling like thunder.

Caught up in the conversation carried from one side of the door to the other, Josey missed when the witch took over her body again. By the time her consciousness caught up with what was happening, she'd already crossed the distance to the door.

"Josey, what're you doing?" Nikki called.

Pushing down the door handle, then pulling it back, Josey heard Murray—whoever Murray might be, club owner, promoter, something—mumble something like "Gentleman here's got a frickin' sword poking in my back." Regaining control, Josey had just enough time to turn back to her friend and say, "It's. . . it's not. . . me. It's the witch."

"Wrong, you're a witch too."

Rebecca's words echoed in the teenager's head.

Then, as the door opened, the screaming began.

CHAPTER TEN

The witch-hunter's journey to the Meeting Hall had been a strange and unsettling experience. After stepping through the witch's circle, Nathaniel Pryce had found himself in a very different Fallen Church than the village he knew so well. At first, he'd believed himself pulled into a new type of Hell. Everything around him was too loud, too bright—an absolute overwhelming of his senses. Even the flooring under his body was not the familiar mud and thatch straw on which he trod daily. Instead, there was a strange, almost mossy covering across it. Only it was too clean to be naturally occurring. The blasphemous ritual candles sat balanced on this material, exuding scents unnatural. By their light, he'd raised his head and found the two witches he'd glimpsed in the woods now staring at him with slack-jawed faces. Each girl was dressed promiscuously, wantonly. *Succubi*, if ever Pryce had seen them.

Indeed, the blatant sinfulness writ large upon their faces awakened the purity in the witch-hunter's heart.

Of that much he was certain. Finding his cutlass and blunderbuss still on his person, Pryce ascertained he'd been whisked away by some unholy magic to an unfamiliar land, but not to Hell. He raised his gun and pulled its trigger, giving notice to the witches that he would be no easy mark for their magics.

Their shrill cries, imitating the yelps of imperiled children, did nothing to sway Pryce from the righteous path. Even as the flames grew at his feet, his skin warming and reddening in their proximity, the witch-hunter focused on his life's mission: eliminating witches. He found further proof of their wicked ways in the appearance of one of the girls. He was near certain he'd seen similar features in the visage of his most recent quarry—Goodwife Rebecca.

Rebecca!

Her wicked name echoed in his head and his heart.

With his weapon reloaded, Pryce fired again. The smoke was thick by then. Some of the fire even managing to penetrate his water-logged clothing. Finding the door to the room blocked—no doubt by the witches, Pryce had but one means of egress from the inferno left.

Cape clutched in his hands, arms crossed over his face as further shielding, he ran at a full-sprint to the window—covered in fine, thick glass, as if something taken from a fanciful European castle—and crashed through the pane.

His fall was short, his landing messy. Pryce permitted himself a single scream, a bellow of inarticulate pain. Then, he bit down on his bottom lip until he tasted the coppery tang of blood. He focused his suffering on that one tiny stinging ache, using that to cast his healing spell.

Eyes rolled back in his head and he spoke the words, using the blood as an offering to demonic forces. Cursing himself for a moment, but letting those feelings of guilt and shame pass from his corporeal form just as quickly.

After all, he reasoned, *I'm doing this, performing these acts, in service to the Lord. I am on a mission most holy and by any means necessary, I must see my good works completed.*

The small price paid, Pryce's body healed and even his clothing was restored to pristine condition. Rising to his feet, both legs as strong as ever, he abandoned the inferno, setting off on a new hunt—both for witches and for answers. He noted the eyes of strangers peering from homes none too dissimilar to the new witches' stronghold. These strangers watched him from the shadows but made no move to confront or hinder his progress.

Good. They must know better than to delay a witch-hunter who's caught a scent most foul and wicked.

* * *

Making slow and steady progress along the tar-blackened roads of what he assumed to be a sinners' paradise, Goodman Pryce heard subtle rumblings, chanting, and clapping sounding from some ways off. Occasionally, he caught glimpses of bright white light beaming onto the ground. Most unnatural. He shivered, assuming a Black Mass was in progress, picturing an assembly of sinners so thick that their mewling entreaties to the Dark Ones were audible even at a distance.

No other souls showed themselves as Pryce continued his hunt, not even the witch-girls who'd fled from him earlier. It wasn't until he came to a tall post, nearly the size of a massive oak tree and crowned with strange gray and black adornments, thick rope-like appendages branching off and connecting to other similar posts along the route that Pryce discovered the broadsheet and his view of where he'd been transported changed.

He tore the page loose from its mooring and brought it close for reading. Lucky for him more of the world's black magic allowed miniature lamps to glow atop curved metallic trees spaced evenly one after the other on the path, illuminating the text. The script was crude, syntax and spelling recognizable as English—though only barely.

Fallen Church WILL BE Y2K-ready!
1999 . . . 2000!

Reading the words a second time, Pryce felt his knees shake and his hand start to tremble.

Fallen Church? Could it be? But in the year of our Lord 1999, the year 2000 nipping at its heels. It seems a shame this corruptible material world has not been brought to an end by this point.

Goodman Pryce began to really study the geography of the strange land in which he'd found himself and discovered it was not so strange after all. He examined signposts, catching sight of familiar names. *There* was where Goodman Owens resided, the path marked for OWENS' ACRE ROAD. And over *there*, the site of a duck pond that once welcomed spry and overtalkative waterfowl now held a strange building marked with golden arches. A sign affixed to the entrance of this glass-enclosed structure read: CLOSED FOR THE GAME.

Peering at the smoky gray of an early evening sky, Pryce shaded his eyes with the tanned leather of his gloves, blocking the unnatural lights surrounding him. These lights glowed too strong. Too intensely.

They are a distraction. A temptation.

Even as he inhaled, breathing in substances foul and rotten as sulfur, Pryce found more layers of deceit to peel away. But once that work was complete and he stared at a moon hanging full and bright over his head, a moon he well-remembered, Pryce grasped the truth in full.

I'm home. Not my home as I remember, but a future version where the sinners have won.

The next thought came easy enough for a man who'd still set himself upon the holy work of witch-hunting.

God the Heavenly Father has sent me here. To redeem

*Fallen Church, to stop the sinners and the witches and all
their foul begotten spawn. This is End of Days and I will be
served as Redeemer.*

Before redemption was possible though, the
witch-hunter knew he'd have to establish a base from
which to launch his cleansing campaign. With his
bearings set, Pryce had one place in mind. One place
where he could go and feel secure.

The Meeting Hall. Located on the outskirts of the
village to protect their assets and records, Pryce had
long conducted his business. He was certain the Hall
would provide sufficient sanctuary.

* * *

The witch-hunter's slow progress across the familiar,
yet corrupted, landscape of Fallen Church was not
without frequent interruptions. Navigating the
labyrinthine rock-hard blackened streets where men,
women, and children of God had once pushed
wooden carts, walked arm-in-arm, and gathered as a
community, proved a difficult task. Buildings larger
than Pryce would've thought possible in the New
World blocked paths and trails he'd once used as
shortcuts. Worse still, when he imagined himself at
the halfway point to the Meeting Hall, terrible, offen-
sively loud roars echoed from behind him. These
guttural cries made the witch-hunter suspect a bear
or a wolf might be on his trail. Or worse, one of the
giant Nephilim, or the beast Leviathan itself risen

from beneath the waves and dragging its swollen carcass onto the land.

Then, a glint of silver, followed by strobing flashes of more bright colors, the swirl racing toward the witch-hunter and then jetting past him just as quickly. Fast, *too fast*. Blues and bloody reds and midnight blacks, each accompanied by twin circles at front and back, all lit like the moon. At the last moment, before he was due to be set upon by these unnaturally fleet vehicles, Pryce dove off the road, rolling to a nearby ditch.

Peeking his head up from his landing spot, his face stained by grass and mud, Pryce caught the tail end of a procession of what he could only describe as armored horseless carriages. *Another false miracle.* One youth, red-faced and wild, blonde hair butter-colored like a sunflower, poked his head out one of the final passing conveyances. The seemingly hale and hearty youth cried out: "Meeting Hall, fellas! Let's gooooooo!"

His yodeling shout was as if made by a savage, a war cry into the night.

However, Goodman Pryce was nearly struck dumb by the words. Could the young men in their magical carts truly be heading to the same destination as he? Once his surroundings returned to quiet, with only the echo of the strangers' passage buzzing in his ears, the man from the past, at last, resumed his journey to the Hall.

* * *

I should've known they'd leave no trace of goodness nor scrap of decency intact in this corrupted future land.

Standing outside another glass edifice, watching a large man in too-tight clothing bleed from his gun-blasted right knee cap and from the gaping red wound carved across the man's neck, the witch-hunter contemplated his next move, while still taking time to enjoy the sinner's writhing on the ground.

What did this ruffian say as I approached him?

'Hey buddy, Halloween was a couple months ago. Gonna need to see some I.D.'

Yet when I spoke my name, surprised that he could even hear me over the throbbing, thrumming rhythmic abominations emanating from within, I was rebuked!

'I.D. Ident-if-i-cation. Show it to me.'

The dying brute of a man clasped a hand across his throat, but there was too much of his gushing serum expelled for that act to make a difference. On his knees, ravaged by the pain of shattered bone and shredded cartilage where the blunderbuss's pellet-riddled blast found its target true, the man collapsed, screaming in agony.

Well, 'tis a lesson he will not soon forget. For the brief remaining time he has on this Earth. . .

Flopping onto his back, whatever final words he might have shared choked back and his every exhalation blood speckled, the man stared up at the witch-hunter, confusion prominent in his features.

When Goodman Pryce had completed his trek through a barren landscape of nightmarish outposts en route to his once-beloved Meeting Hall, he'd found horseless chariots, the same ones that'd passed him earlier, sitting idle and empty in a sea of black. He'd followed the path to its inevitable end. But what waited for him there was not the Meeting Hall he expected or remembered.

Having dispatched the guardian at the gates of this hellish mockery of Fallen Church's former sanctuary and worship hall, the witch-hunter hardened his heart and entered the palace of sin. His boot left its heavy tread across the ruined throat of the now-dead sinful doorman. Pryce's resultant bloody footprints would mark his journey into the depths of Hell.

* * *

Inside the building, the assault on his senses was all-encompassing. Flashing lights, like will o' the wisps gone mad, made erratic circles before his eyes. Too much screaming and howling, growling, all of these noises seemingly meant to serve as music. This was not the music of the spheres, but a chorus of the damned. Pockets and pools of darkness flooded the space, giving cover to the sinners present. Additional purple-hued lights pulsed at the feet of all. Similar lights lined the upper portions of the walls, strung up close to the ceiling.

In some sections, mirrors replaced the usual ceiling material. Pryce gazed up at his reflection amid the chaos. He saw the Hell-World reversed, turned upside down. *As above, so below.*

The stench of sexual awakening, of foul bodies in gyrating motion, nearly knocked the witch-hunter to his knees when he'd fully breathed it in. Head on a swivel, he looked for a source and first located an assembly of men, many young, a few old, imbibing suspect beverages, sweating in their seats, laughing like braying donkeys.

The same curly-haired towheaded young man who'd issued a rallying cry to his peers, inviting them to this bastardized version of the Meeting Hall, leaned forward with paper scrip in hand, thrusting the offering onto a platform upon which false lights in the Hall were focused.

A wanton harlot.

Hardly wearing anything at all, the woman on the platform was painted in pinks and purples, her bosom heaving, hips spread wide in a most sinful manner. She danced and gyrated up to the edge of the stage. There, she bent down and snatched up the young man's offering. It was sinful. Ungodly.

But Goodman Pryce could not look away.

"Want a private dance, stranger?"

The whispered cooing so close to his person drew Pryce's attention from the stage. His reaction to what stood before him was immediate, visceral. The witch-hunter felt his eyes bulging against the sockets even more than usual, his fleshy lips trembling into a snarl.

It was a woman.

Clad in undergarments, decadent ones at that, just like the strumpet on the stage, this new woman ran pale fingers up and down the length of Pryce's glove-clad arm. He stole a glance down and found her bosom slick with sweat, glittering most unnaturally.

"You won't need these gloves with me, baby. You can touch me *all* over. Xenia's gonna take real good care of you." Then, touching the barrel of his blunder-buss, she added, "I'll make sure *all* your guns go off."

She licked her lips. Performing. Going through a well-rehearsed routine. Pryce considered her an illusion, a thought-form given life to serve as a distraction.

From the witches...

Cutlass at his side, he brought his gloved hand to the temptress's face and shoved her away. Hard. He half-expected her to burst into a cloud of hornets or dissipate as if some foul cloud of gas.

On the stage, the other woman continued dancing, removing her garments as well. The men watching paid no mind to the witch-hunter's confrontation. They were under the spell of the woman performing.

But Pryce's actions had not gone entirely unno-ticed. A short, stocky, sweaty man, golden chains dangling from his neck and hair on his shoulders peeking through the ragged neck of his shirt, made a beeline for the witch-hunter. "Alright, pal, I dunno how or why Maurice let you in here, but you do *not* mess with my girls, capiche?"

He was a troll of a man. Sloppy, unfit, and

unsound. It was nothing for Pryce to draw his blade and nick a quick sharp slice into the man's cheek. He then ignored the way his would-be verbal assaulter burst into tears, holding a hand to his bleeding face. Instead, the witch-hunter returned his attention to the girl, the one he believed was sent as a witch's distraction. She fled from the chaos of the building's main meeting space, heading for a backroom in the establishment.

The man he'd cut sank to his knees, but Pryce grabbed him by the open collar of his shirt, forcing him to stand.

"Take me to the witches," he commanded. His voice boomed above the music, the laughter and the sin, each word imbued with Godly power. Goodman Pryce would not be disobeyed.

CHAPTER ELEVEN

The strange man that they'd accidentally summoned from Fallen Church's past— *Goodman Pryce, his name was. . . is Goodman Nathaniel Pryce*, and Josey knew *this* because her ancestor, who they'd intended to contact, still floated around inside her head, telling her everything about the man and his cruel intentions—pressed the wide-mouthed barrel of his ancient firearm to the back of the sweat-slicked head of the trembling strip club owner he'd used as cover to access the dancers' dressing room. Without hesitation, Pryce pulled the trigger, sending a spray of pellets from the gun that eviscerated the club owner's face from front to back.

Josey retreated a half-step, expecting the spray to carry forward hitting her in the face as well, extinguishing her life as it'd just done to the club owner.

Instead, outside of her conscious control, her hands waved in a highly specific sequence. As the life she'd seen flashing before her eyes faded away still incomplete, she noted a glowing blue-tinted energy

signature crackling from between her palms and
extending beyond her person. This translucent blue
light proved solid enough to ensnare the fragments of
gunpowder and shot, along with the bone and skin
scraps from the dead man, stopping all forward
motion and holding these elements in place.

"Now, let go."

Her ancestor's words, spoken in Josey's voice,
served as both command and release. She thrust her
hands forward, palms toward the witch-hunter. The
cloud of pellet spray reversed course, and was
launched with even greater force back at Goodman
Pryce.

The witch-hunter twitched his head to the side
unnaturally quick. His face was in the path of shrapnel
one moment, then clear the next. In less than the blink
of an eye. He moved that fast. Josey noted an after-
image of the man's face, dissipating like red-tinted
smoke when struck by the shot. The phantom's
features curled into a rage-filled snarl.

With the spell of this uncanny moment broken,
chaos followed quickly.

More screams echoed from the club floor. Josey
was certain she heard Ashton and some of the other
football players among those shouting, panicking. "Yo!
Is this for real? Is that blood? Like for real?!"

From the rear of the dressing room, Nikki's sister
DiDi attempted to keep order among the other dancers
—soothing them, while also looking for a plan of
action, a way to get everyone out and safe. She had the

backdoor open, and was waving, urging the other girls to make their escape. "Come on!" she shouted. "We gotta get the *hell* outta here."

DiDi clearly understood it was not the time to hesitate or mince words.

Josey, however, remained frozen in the doorway between the dressing room and the main floor. Her shoes were stained with blood at the toes. *At least it's not my own.* The lights from the club still flashed, on and off, purples, pinks, neon greens, and icy blues. Their rapid-fire changing made it difficult to see what was happening in the main room.

Where did Pryce go?

Josey wasn't sure if the thought was hers or that of her ancestor. Nor did she think it mattered.

Behind her, someone was crying. A hand grabbed for Josey's. She flinched, but settled when she saw it was Nikki. Surprisingly, Nikki was the one sobbing, her hitched breaths following each expulsion of tears.

"We. . . we. . . we need to. . ."

Before her friend finished her plea and pulled Josey through the back exit and out to a parking lot filled with fleeing dancers, the tumult outside the dressing room drew to a immediate silence—followed shortly by a sudden, unmistakable, hacking and slicing combination. These sounds were accompanied the snarl of the witch-hunter.

The severed head—belonging to one of their school's football players—soared through the kaleidoscopic club-lit semidarkness and landed with a *splat* at Josey's feet. Nikki and Josey held onto each other, somehow managing to keep themselves upright. The dumbfounded expression forever etched on the dead boy's face unsettled Josey's stomach. She gagged.

With no time to turn aside or swallow it back, she barfed, spraying the mozzarella sticks and marinara sauce she'd split with Nikki prior to the summoning— a moment that seemed a lifetime ago. It splattered the coat and tunic of the witch-hunter, who was already returned. raising his cutlass above his head, preparing for another strike.

"Foul witch!" he growled, before lunging into the dressing room, swinging his sword back and forth. He swung one way and the girls dove to the other side to avoid the sweeping arc of the blade. It smashed against the mirror glass above one table, sending silver shards everywhere. The witch-hunter seethed with rage and pain, white, foamy spittle speckling from between his clenched teeth.

Josey and Nikki clasped hands and ran for the exit, the friends moving in tandem.

But they weren't fast enough. Pryce's sword-wielding hand, now studded with mirror-glass, slashed the weapon before the thin space just shy of their faces. "You," he said, speaking to Josey. "You are of the witch's bloodline. I feel her presence within you."

Facing the panicked and stunned faces of the two girls, he added, "Did you think you could hide from me, Rebecca? All this while knowing that I was the one who taught you how?"

Taught you how?

Never mind that, Josephine! Rebecca's voice came as a shouted command inside Josey's head, the words echoing in her skull. The force of the witch's voice was painful to experience this way, forcing Josey to drop her friend's hand and clutch at the sides of her head.

Blood, deep red and potent, dribbled from Josey's nose, ears, and even her eyes.

"Josey, are you—" Nikki's question was cut short, as Pryce rushed forward. Instead of finishing her query, Nikki only had a moment to pull her friend away, moving them deeper into the dressing room, closer to the still open exit.

Luckily for the duo, Pryce's forward motion was *not* of his own accord. After crashing to the floor, nearly missing having a spiked stiletto heel impaled through one of his eyes, the witch-hunter found himself covered by a scrum of football players, their jerseys still on but with blood now as prevalent as grass stains and spilled celebratory beers.

Ashton Gore raised his head from the center of the pile-on. Eyes wide, lips chapped, giving Josey the impression that underage boozing might not have been the only illicit activity the footballers were engaged in that evening, Ashton rallied his teammates one more time. "Let's kick this Pilgrim Dude's ass!"

He and the other jocks rained down punches and delivered swift kicks to Pryce's prone form. A linebacker's foot came down hard on the stranger's sword-wielding hand. The crunch of newly-shattered bones went off like a gunshot in the dressing room. The sword slid from Pryce's grasp.

Josey found herself reaching for the abandoned weapon.

However, realizing she wasn't in control of her body, or her actions, she forced herself to stop.

No, she thought, addressing the other presence within her mind, *I won't let you control me like this. Not until you...*

Girl, you are as big a fool as I was when Pryce slithered his unholy way into my presence...

Before, Josey could fire back or defend herself or ask just what the hell Rebecca meant by all that, Nikki pulled on her again, dragging her toward the exit. DiDi was still there, her fear and confusion evident, but her protective spirit covering for both of those emotions.

As Nikki and Josey escaped the dressing room, the girl with the witch inside her head made brief eye contact with Ashton, her longtime bully and tormentor turned inadvertent rescuer. His hands were bruising, his face already red and flushed. "Witch Bitch?" he asked with a strange smile crossing his lips.

Then, perhaps realizing it didn't much matter *why* or *how* the strange Goth girls from his school had got there, he shouted, "Get outta here! We'll take care of the freak."

A new crackling energy signature appeared, similar to the blue light Josey manifested earlier. This

time, crimson radiated from Pryce's body and penetrated the tattered remnants of his cloak, putting the
lie to Ashton's statement.

As Josey was yanked by Nikki and her sister into
the back lot, the heavy door slamming shut behind
them, she watched the red light becoming a physical
presence, blood-red fingers lifting Ashton and the
other would-be heroes and then throwing them about
helter-skelter.

* * *

The door was closed before her. The witch-hunter and
his unnatural powers were out of sight, the grunting of
their town's gridiron heroes and the smack of fists
against the woolen clothes of the man out of time, all
were gone to silence. It took Josey another moment to
reorient herself, to get used to the new forms of chaos
that awaited her outside the club.

More screaming and shouting filled the parking
lots, both front and back, punctuated by the clatter of
heels against the asphalt or the squeal of tires on the
fleeing dancers' and patrons' vehicles.

"Josey!"

There was Nikki, already in her bug, with DiDi
waiting by the passenger side, ready to let Josey climb
in first.

Josey looked from the closed door that led into the
club and back to her friends. Behind them, in the
distance, the night sky was lit up blue and white and

red in spiraling patterns. Police sirens squealed to match this light show.

"We have to. . ."

We have to flee. You are not ready for what must be done, Rebecca said inside Josey's head. Her voice was curt, almost sounding disdainful.

Moving toward Nikki's car, Josey felt this burden of disappointment inside and out. She was tired, her body aching and her mind a raging storm. For a long while, when it came to her family—what they wanted for her, what they wished her to be, she'd felt herself failing to live up to those expectations. She'd felt like she was never enough, never exactly what they wanted.

It hurt worse when it was her ancestor, an *actual witch* and someone she believed would actually understand her, who was the one passing judgment.

In silence, she climbed into the backseat and buckled up, letting DiDi take the front passenger seat next to her sister. Then, Nikki sped from the parking lot and pulled onto the service road, passing a police car heading the opposite direction, to the strip club and the witch-hunter rampaging inside.

The blue light shone on Josey for a moment but her eyes were cast down to her lap. Staring at her hands. Opening and closing them, trying to find a spark of magical power still there.

Finding nothing, she felt more powerless than ever before.

CHAPTER TWELVE

W hat was it the tow-headed one called the Wesley descendant? Ah, yes, "Witch Bitch," that is what he said. How crass, how vulgar. . . how delightfully appropriate. I suppose I'll let that boy live. For now. But as for these other roustabouts. . .

Turning thought into action, Goodman Pryce imagined a mighty hand, an oversized appendage of an angry God, flexing and squeezing tight around the bodies of the sinners. The crimson aura he'd generated wrapped tendrils tighter and tighter around those young men who'd moments before assaulted the witch-hunter with zealous fervor. *There is rage in these young men, perhaps something to harness, to redirect.*

But Pryce pushed those notions aside for the moment, thinking, *No, no spare the rod and spoil the child. An example must be made.*

Even as Pryce's body healed, his bruises fading, skin and bones stitching themselves back together, the young men's ribs cracked, their hearts burst, and their lungs exploded. The power coursing through Pryce allowed him to treat his attackers as nothing more than some child's cornhusk dolls.

Rising to his feet, brushing himself clean, Pryce gave a nod, recalling the manifested power back into his mortal form. The dead boys fell at his feet. All that remained was the one living young man, down on his knees, muttering prayers, pleading for forgiveness. A broken, humbled man-child. It made the witch-hunter smile to see the arrogant lad brought low. He stepped closer, his gloved hand taking the boy's chin and forcing him to look up into the face of the one who'd spared him.

"Wh—what. . . what *are you* supposed to be?" the boy asked, his confusion and fear prominently displayed.

"I am the witch-hunter and my night's work is just beginning," Pryce said.

"Freeze!"

The shouted command came like a cur's bark from across the main hall.

Uniformed men, seemingly armored for war, aimed strange devices that somewhat resembled weapons, guns even, at Pryce and the young man in his grasp. There was an air of authority, of power about these new personages. *And beneath that power, the same untapped rage I sensed in the ruffians previously.* Like recognizing like, Pryce released the young man and held his hands up in the air, slow and cautious. Making it clear that he meant no harm and would come peacefully to wherever they might wish to take him.

It was a calculated move. Pryce sensed there was still much to learn about this future version of Fallen Church. As the witch-hunter, he could be patient. He'd wait and watch and learn, gathering the necessary intelligence to maneuver his quarry to exactly where he wanted them.

* * *

Later, Pryce sat stiff-backed and still in the rear of the justice of the peace's horseless carriage. The vehicle appeared to have magic torches attached to its thick, purring metal roof, swirling blue and white beams across the night sky. The uniformed man, acting as escort, sat in the conveyance's forward compartment, separated from Pryce by a physical barrier. It'd taken two of the other uniformed men, working in tandem, to harness the witch-hunter into the cotton-soft seatback of the carriage. Something they kept calling a "car."

Other men had taken Pryce's weapons. With hands cuffed behind his back, he had not missed the raised eyebrows and whispered questions the men shared about his appearance and his righteous instruments. But he'd stayed quiet. Nodding or shaking his head, depending on what he was asked. He made no mention of the year from which he'd come or of witches, warlocks, and other corrupted powers. These future men only thought of him as a stranger. A violent stranger, yes. But still, just a stranger. He was content to keep their opinion of him limited in this manner.

I can be strange without being out of place. I can show them the purity of my heart, my intentions, and my holy mission.

Voices emerged, garbled and crackling, from the front of the carriage. Strangely, the uniformed man, turning a wheel and moving the vehicle by doing so, sat with lips closed. It was as though he communed with a demonic, otherworldly presence.

"All units. All units. Be advised, we are looking for a Volkswagen Bug. License plate. . ."

Wrists bound behind his back, hands too close together so he couldn't properly make a sigil, Pryce had to settle for listening and absorbing more information. It was an easy enough thing for him to do. While he was a witch-hunter first and foremost, the heart of a scholar also beat within his chest.

He'd learned under the tutelage of great minds— from men, women, and things that dwelled in the shadows left by hellfire's wake. These mentors were without mercy, without compassion, without pity, and they'd passed those traits to Pryce.

". . . vehicle's believed to hold Josephine 'Josey' Wesley and Nikki Farr, students at Fallen Church High School, both wanted for further questioning concerning a recent house fire at the Wesleys' home on the 1200 block of. . ."

To their understanding, witch's spawn has been quite busy this evening.

". . . with Denise Dianna "DiDi" Farr, 27, an employee of the Meeting Hall and sister of Nikki. Proceed with caution. You all know how the Farrs can be."

The last part made Pryce laugh. Even as the metal cuffs chafed the skin of his wrists, he threw his head back, unleashing a continuous stream of guffaws.

"Hey! Hey!" The lawman sitting up front, bashed a fist against the mesh screen separating himself from his prisoner. "Shut up back there!"

Then, the officer picked something up from the front of his vehicle and pressed down on a button.

Hearing his laughter bounced back, Pryce paused. *There's magic in this future world*, he thought, *much more than I could've imagined. So much to learn, to master.*

And all the time in this world to do it in. . . perhaps I should stay. . .

The angry, uniformed lawman spoke to the seem- ingly demonic voices issuing from the front of his vehicle.

"Dispatch, I'm en route to the precinct with pris- oner in tow. Some of the others involved in the, uh, incident are heading that way in McGregor's squad car. You tell 'em to throw that Gore kid in the drunk tank and let him sleep it off. . . I know his Daddy'd want that. Somethin' to keep his boy scared straight."

Hearing this strange conversation, Pryce considered how he'd started his day in the year 1693 and somehow wound up in the year 1999.

"Is it truly 1900 and 99?" he asked.

Releasing his grip on the strange speaking device, the officer's eyes flashed with questions of its own into the mirror above his seat. "Yeah," he said. "But why do you say it like that?"

Pryce ignored the critique of his word choice and continued. "So that means the new millennium's dawning. Are you not afraid of what's to come?"

"What? Afraid? You kidding me, pal?" The lawman's protests petered off, revealing more of his heart's truth than he might've liked.

They continued in silence for a few more moments, past a few more streets familiar but different to the witch-hunter.

Then, the officer spoke again. "They say we'll be okay. Tell us the computers won't crash or shut down or whatever. Say it'll be like any other day. But. . . that's not how it feels. Feels like we're past due for something bad to happen. Something we've maybe earned."

"Judgment Day," the witch-hunter said.

From the back, Pryce watched the other man slowly nodding.

"Yeah, yeah," the lawman said, "like we learned in Sunday School. Judgment freakin' Day."

Pryce smiled, relieved to be connecting with a Godly man, or at the very least one who appeared to aspire to such ways. "Pardon me, sir," he said, "but would you mind sharing your Christian name with me? I am Nathaniel Pryce and I am here to do the Lord's work."

CHAPTER THIRTEEN

At last, Josey had got her way, and they were going to the Farrs' house. However, their stay there didn't seem likely to last long. She, Nikki, and DiDi had pulled to the curb in front of their house, tires crunching over broken, neglected asphalt, when the front door slammed open. Nikki's mom Linda stormed outside in a Tweety Bird nightshirt, with a worn-thin olive green bathrobe over that, pink rollers in her hair, and a cigarette dangling ash balanced on her bottom lip. "Nuh-uh," she said, making sure to lock eyes with each girl as she stomped across the porch and down the cracked and splintering wooden steps.

"They got everybody all over town looking for you. I heard it on the police band," she said.

It shook Josey a bit, to think of Mrs. Farr on her couch or lying in her bed, listening to the coded back-and-forth dialogues between dispatchers and officers. But when she considered the legal troubles their family had had since moving to Fallen Church and the fact that their little brother was currently in juvie and her dad "taking some time away," Josey supposed there was some sense to it.

DiDi took the lead, continuing to walk toward the house, on a collision course with her mother. "Mama," she said, "give us a break, okay? Do you even know what just happened back there. . ."

The older woman stood with hands on hips, the yellow cartoon bird thrust forward as further warning. "They got that girl's house burnt down with them two fleeing the scene," she said, pointing to Nikki and Josey in rapid succession. "Then, they got a heap of dead folks at that damn club of yours, and the Wesley girl throwing bullets at strangers or something, couldn't tell for sure the way they were talkin' about it on the radio. . ."

"But that wasn't—" Josey started to protest, but felt her ancestor stirring inside. Worn out, exhausted, finding herself facing *yet another* obstacle in a long night of obstacles, Josey relented to Rebecca's control.

Fine, she thought, *you wanna take over? Be my guest.*

No, Rebecca said, speaking within the girl's mind. *If you want this sanctuary, then it's you who will have to earn it. Open your mind and heart and soul to the power. . ."*

"I don't know if I can. . ."

"Who's she talking to?" Linda asked, paranoia and fear present in each syllable.

Nikki took Josey's hand. The redhead girl, the one she couldn't stop thinking of—no matter how hard she tried, no matter how sure she was that the feelings she held for her friend would only lead to more bullying, more torment, more *everything awful*—gave her a squeeze.

"Whatever it is, you can do it," Nikki said.

Her words and the nervous smile following were all the permission Josey needed. She took a deep breath and directed her next thought to her ancestor inside her head. *Okay, show me how to fix this. Teach me what to do.*

Rebecca began the lesson: *First, make the connection. Your body and the other's and the earth at your feet.*

Josey slid her shoes off her feet, her socks came next. The ground was cold, with dead grass crunching under the soles of her feet. She walked forward, doing her damnedest to fake confidence, to appear as nonchalant and casual as she could. An impossible task most days for a teenage girl, much more so on that chaotic evening.

However Josey managed it, Linda seemed convinced enough to remain in place, not backing up or offering protests at the young woman's approach. At least not until it was too late.

"Hold on, what do you think you're. . ."

Then, Josey put her hand on the woman's round, flushed cheek. All at once, the girl's mouth formed an "o," as she saw colors swirling around her and Mrs.

Farr, mist-like threads connecting the ground to her body and her body to the other woman's. In most cases, the threads appeared as a vibrant cornucopia of colors, a rainbow coalition of mystical forces. But in other spots, black and gray, desiccated strands amassed.

You must harvest the dark energies. Take them into yourself. Free this woman of her burden. As witches, that is what we do. That is what our powers are meant for. . .

Listening to her ancestor's directions, Josey took her free hand and reached for the dark strands emanating from her friend's mother. As her fingertips approached the glowing, wispy tendrils, they transformed into solid matter, becoming thick rope-like extensions she could wrap her hand around.

Josey pulled back on these growths, tearing away the darkness. Once they were ripped free from her body, Linda's eyes rolled back white. The immediate, overpowering stink of sulfur made Josey's nostrils wrinkle. Her eyes watered. But somehow, as if she'd accessed some in-born trait, a genetic supernatural legacy passed down through generations, she found herself certain about what was needed next.

And this, without Rebecca having to say a word.

Josey opened her mouth and stuffed the solidified darkness inside. Chewing, slurping, biting, ignoring the bilious taste and the sting of the matter as it resisted her attempts at consumption. Even after the copper tang of freshly-spilled blood filled her mouth, Josey would not stop. When the darkness was fully inside her, Josey's hand fell from the older woman's cheek and she collapsed to the ground. She retched, both hands now clutching her stomach. The energy, the primary color bouquet she'd witnessed earlier, faded away.

Only you can see the energy. Rebecca's voice was a whisper in the young woman's mind.

Nikki and DiDi were at her side, checking to make sure she was okay.

Josey shuddered, a cold sweat breaking out on her forehead. But even as the feverish chill washed over her, she still managed to roll on her back and look up into the face of her friend's mother.

Linda's anger and fear were gone without a trace —as if they'd never been there at all. She bent down to assist her daughters in helping Josey to her feet. "There, there," the woman said, speaking in a soothing tone that reminded Josey of watching Mr. Rogers when she was a kid. The gentleness, the acceptance, the notion that everyone had a place, a purpose. That everyone mattered. All of that now came through in the eldest Farr's speech

"I'm so sorry," Linda continued. "I don't know what came over me. You all come on in from the cold and get warmed up."

Finally, noticing how her teeth chattered, Josey's adrenaline spike faded and the realization of just how cold it was settled over her. She and Nikki were far from the inferno of her home and of the sex-scented body-heat intensity in the Meeting Hall. They were standing outside on an early winter evening in New England. As if on-cue, a sharp wind whistled down the street and the shadowed trees on the block, bare except for their final few stubborn leaves, bent in supplication.

* * *

Moments later, inside the tiny house that Nikki and her family called home, with the space made even tighter by the shipping boxes containing drunkenly-purchased QVC kitchen gadgets, amassed piles of old newspapers and TV Guides, and the crushed remnants of too many beer cans and cigarette packs and pizza boxes, all coalescing in a hoarder's paradise, Josey sat upright and still on a worn-in couch with a scratchy woolen throw blanket pulled to her chin and a mug that smelled not-so-faintly of bourbon, but that was currently filled with hot tea, clutched between her hands.

Taking another slow sip of the warm, lemon-scented tea, Josey looked up from the mug to find Linda standing before her, still beaming with a smile. It was odd, seeing Nikki's mom smiling that much. As if reading her friend's mind, Nikki plopped down—not on the other end of the couch but right beside Josey. She leaned in close, doing her best to ignore her mother's blissed-out smile. "What the hell did you do to her?" she asked.

Josey opened her mouth, ready to fire off a snappy

comeback, engaging in the kind of back-and-forth banter she was used to with her friend. But the expression on Nikki's face suggested that the time for jokes was past.

"I . . . I . . . I think I helped her. At least, that's what. . . Rebecca says."

Nikki arched an eyebrow again. "Really?" she said. "Is that what the *witch* told you?"

"Hey, I. . ."

Josey felt something stirring inside, a shivering sensation different from the winter chill experienced moments earlier outside the house. It was Rebecca, she knew, trying again to assert herself. But Josey was ready this time. As her ancestor had droned on with lessons shared from the black magic spell books in which *she'd* been instructed, her descendant had seemingly picked up more than she'd first believed. The same way she'd been able to ace Algebra II despite skipping over half of the classes to work on art projects in Mr. Mundy's classroom/studio. Josey had picked up just enough to get by.

Imagine a doorway in front of the Other.

Imagine a door.

Now, close the door.

She cut her ancestor off, thinking, *Sorry, Rebecca, but I can handle this.*

A gentle pounding followed for a moment, the witch-spirit's efforts half-hearted, noncommittal. Then, she stopped.

Alright girl, Rebecca thought at her descendant,

this is your business to handle. But be quick, for time is running out and the witch-hunter will not be so easily delayed or detained.

Seeming to sense that whatever internal back-and-forth going on inside her friend's head had reached a détente, Nikki spoke next. "What are we supposed to do now?" she asked her friend.

There it was. The million dollar question.

Before anyone in the Farr's filthy living room could offer a suggestion, the click of the family's rotary phone being returned to its cradle drew all attention to DiDi as she stood in the narrow space between the living room and the family's equally cluttered kitchen.

"We can't stay here long," she said. "None of us. Not us, not Mama, not. . ."

As if hearing the fear in her older daughter's voice had somehow broken the spell, Linda moved to DiDi's side. "What's wrong? What the hell's going on now?"

Josey sat on the couch, turning her head to stare at the front entryway of the house. In that moment, she was certain that a new vision had struck her, pulling her from the present and showing something from "what had been." She wondered if her witch ancestor bore responsibility for these resurrected sights and sounds and smells, all of her senses assailed at once. The squish of muddy, unpaved earth under feet. The smell of burning and horse manure on the wind.

A floating assemblage of tiny flames and some not-so-tiny flames bounced before her eyes, visible through—but dulled by—the window glass in the foyer. Outside, screams and shouts grew louder and louder, as though whatever or whoever made the noise was moving closer and closer—and bringing the fire with them.

Again, she thought of another vision, the same one she'd had in the third grade. Her skin prickled as if touched all over by the same intense heat that manifested when she'd seen her ancestor burnt at the stake. She felt Rebecca. Angry, defiant. Betrayed. The far-off past overlapped with the present, soon becoming the ancient past overlapping with experiences from centuries more immediate, all of these timelines double exposed across Josey's here and now.

"Do you see it too?"

It surprised Josey to hear the question coming from Nikki. It shocked her that much more when the other two Farrs nodded as well.

Outside, the entirety of the Fallen Church High student body marched toward that small house on the bad side of town. Everyone appeared as if they'd come fresh from the game or maybe from a house party or bonfire held afterward. In their Letterman jackets, their cheerleading sweaters and skirts, in parkas, in blue jeans, in Tommy Hilfiger and Starter jacket ensembles, in JNCOs with wallet chains, in oversized tees over waffle-print pattern long john henleys. The jocks, the cheerleaders, the stoners, the band geeks, the theater kids, some normally nice, unassumingly bland kids, and others who only pretended to be that way.

Seemingly everyone from the student body approached from outside. Everyone except Josey and Nikki. And Josey's brother who she imagined was still with her parents.

All of the marchers shared two points connecting them together, two traits that bound them. First, each person carried a makeshift wooden torch in their hands. The fiery pieces of scrap ranged from skinny near twig-like branches to thick logs seemingly impossible for one person to carry unless they were a member of the school's more athletic set. The Fallen Church High students carried these torches, lighting up the night, appearing more like the angry mob in one of the old black-and-white monster flicks than pep rally attendees.

Rising from the couch, moving toward the front of the house, Josey grew more and more certain that the other shared trait she saw among her classmates was an illusion, a falsehood. It could not be true! Perhaps it was nothing more than a trick of the light. But it was no overexposed film, no photograph in need of digital retouching, moving closer and closer to the Farrs' abode. Boys and girls, young men and young women, each member of the mob baying for blood, chanting "witch bitch, witch bitch, witch bitch. . ." over and over, seemed to have eyes that glowed unnaturally red. Not bloodshot or crimson-tinged with irritation, these eyes glimmered, crackling with a hellish and unholy power.

Unlike the mystical energy she'd learned to

harness under the witch's instruction, this red—
seemingly empowered by the flames the students
wielded—was something else entirely. Not just a
warning or cautionary symbol, it was the danger itself,
and its collision course with Josey appeared unavoid-
able. Inevitable.

CHAPTER FOURTEEN

The witch-hunter stayed silent for as long as he could. He'd found silence worked in his favor. It certainly had in the Fallen Church—*his* Fallen Church—of the 1600s, from the moment he'd come to the small village in the New Hampshire colony with eyes and ears open and mouth closed. Doing so allowed him to pick up on the displeasure of the yeoman farmers who thought their annual crops less than what they'd expected, or on the discord between neighbors still sore about the proximity of their lodgings on the ships as they were transported across the mighty Atlantic, or on the whispered gossip about a young woman living alone at the outskirts of town, a beautiful free spirit who sought answers beyond the weekly sermons given at the village meeting hall.

It was simple enough—to create a witch for *them* and for himself, the witch-hunter.

How lucky then, Pryce believed, to have passed through the summoning circle and emerged to a Fallen

Church in the last days of the 1900s, and to discover the need for witch *and witch-hunter* as strong as it'd ever been.

So, he'd kept silent for the majority of his capture. He'd picked out voices from the cacophony that greeted him and the man who'd taken him in the horseless carriage—*Officer Miller, the gentleman's name is Officer Miller*—when they'd arrived at this "station." He caught muttered phrases, varying halves of conversations, all from other uniformed and armed men and even a few women (*of all things*).

"Swear to God..."

"Some folks, Tom Turner, Barney Watters, the Jonesy Twins, other neighbors of the Wesley girl, they've been out looking for 'em since those girls ran from her burnt down house. Chief said to tell 'em..."

"Got all them whor... 'scuse me, ladies, crying, screaming keeping everybody up at the ER. They're in the clinic now, checking on one of their own who got shot. Got one of 'em, one of her, y'knows, blasted off. Yeah... silicone or whatever went everywhere. Not so sexy now. Heh."

"Hey Jenkins, we got a call from Old Man Tolliver about some of the high schoolers out... having a kegger at... yeah that's what I told him. We got bigger things to worry about tonight."

The groan, starting low and rising in intensity, halted the witch-hunter's absorption of this gossip and hearsay. Wrapping his hands around the bars of his cell, he called out to whoever moaned nearby.

"Who's there?"

The sound reached its crescendo, a young man's frustrated wail echoing off the walls of what sounded like another near-empty cell next to the one where they'd placed Pryce. Then, a voice, quivering and terrified spoke up, ". . . kill me," a half-sentence, devoid of additional context.

Pryce recognized the voice, however. It belonged to the blond man-child. *What had the others called him? Ashton.*

Ashton was of an age where he should already have had a plot of land, a wife, and a brood of children, where he should be giving back to his community. Instead, Pryce found him as a wanton child, shirking all responsibilities, living only for his gluttonous, lustful pleasures. Given the stark, barren conditions, all cold metals and concrete, of his own cell, the witch-hunter was not surprised to hear the young man sounding as broken-down as he did.

"What's that, boy?" he asked.

From next door came more sounds of sniveling, gasping breaths emerging from the young man's mouth as he cried, while also trying to stop long enough to answer the question. Finally, Ashton managed to say, "My dad's gonna kill me."

Pryce wanted to laugh. *Such a childish complaint.*

However, he knew there was more work to be done, and that these future times differed from the period he'd been living through before this summoning.

"No, child, no, no," he said in a soothing voice.

"You don't understand," Ashton continued. "He doesn't know about the club. He's a. . . a. . . prayerful man. Doesn't know anything about what me and the boys do. He. . . he. . . thinks I go and pray with the team after the game. I told him. . ."

"A lie?"

No answer to Pryce's query came from the other cell. Only more sniffling, sobs swallowed back with a whine at the end as punctuation.

"How many lies have you told?" Pryce asked.

More silence.

"Sin is a burden we carry in our hearts, lad. It weighs us down from the inside."

"I don't. . . I don't. . ." The young man struggled to get his words out.

Pryce switched strategies, turning to clucking, cooing, as if addressing a newborn babe or a simple-minded servant. "There, there, there, there," he said.

"I have. . ." The boy stopped, as if processing a wave of new information, his fractured memories of the Meeting Hall only now returning in fits and starts.

That was another trick Pryce had learned, the ability to cloud the minds of those who might bear witness to his *powers*. An imperfect spell, but one that got the job done well enough.

"Nooooooo!" the young man moaned again. "You killed them. You killed those people. My friends. The girls. . ."

"Those were no girls," Pryce said.

The boy's former cocksure confidence was

stripped away, leaving him a hollow shell. "They were. They were. . ."

"*Witches*," Pryce said.

"No, that's not. . . that's not true."

Pryce endured another jag of sobbing and hyperventilating from the young man. While doing so, he brought a finger to his lips, catching one of his long, yellowed nails between his teeth. He bit down until he heard a satisfying *crunch*, then twisted his finger this way and that. Finally, part of the nail came loose. He spit it back into his palm, and considered the jagged-edged crescent resting against his pasty flesh.

With the first part of the work complete, Pryce continued his interrogation, his slow, meticulous breaking-down of his target. "There are many here with us, many of our fellow citizens, who'd call those women 'witches,' and worse, yes? I've heard them and I'm certain you have as well. Answer me, boy!"

As though the witch-hunter had stepped through the wall separating their cells and slapped him in the face, Ashton blurted out his answer. "Ye. . . yes."

"And your friends? Your companions? They've called them worse names?"

"Yes."

"But they—and *you*—still traveled to that den of sin and depravity?"

The boy's next *yes* was nearly drowned out by choking sobs. Hearing them, a smile spread across the witch-hunter's face. He set the fingernail fragment on the cell floor and waved his hands over it, mumbling in another tongue. Between those unnatural syllables, he also still managed to continue his taunting of the boy who'd dared defy him.

"You've let your father down."

"No, I . . ."

"Don't lie. You've let your father down."

"I have. . . I. . . yes."

"You've let your family down. *Say it.*"

"I've let my family down."

Pryce's pale skin and watery eyes lit up with a reddish hue. It slowly expanded across his white body, as his magic worked its way through him and onto the ragged clipping. He watched as the cutting morphed and shifted, growing in size.

Pryce recalled how Rebecca Wesley once lay beside him in the grass, looking at the stars with him, and asking how he could claim to be a religious man while invoking the entities who powered his workings. Communing with beings that some might call devils.

He knew the answer he gave then still applied in this strange, unexpected "future-present" in which he'd found himself.

"These names are all in Scripture. Is not our Holy Bible the Word of God? Then, are these words, these names, not part of that Word, not part of God?"

"What'd you say?" Ashton asked, nearly breaking the witch-hunter's concentration.

But the spell work was nearly finished and Pryce prided himself on being quick on his feet, clever in the face of adversity.

"They rushed you into the cell, didn't they?" he asked the boy with a dominance-asserting growl.

"Yes," the boy answered.

"You have a belt still?"

"Yes."

"What will they think of you? Your father? Your family? Your neighbors? Every pure soul in Fallen Church?"

His questions came one after another, like the crack of a cat-o'-nine-tails against a penitent's back. Pryce pictured the boy squirming, stung by the implications of each query.

He didn't need answers. Ashton didn't need to say a word, either confirming or denying what the witch-hunter said. Pryce only needed to hear the clink of a buckle coming undone under the boy's nerve-wracked ministrations. Then, the sound of the leather strap pulled quickly through belt loops, the buckle clinking again as burnished golden pieces smacked against each other.

A grunt of exertion. The leather slapping against a metal pipe jutting from the upper portion of the wall, in a spot where it met the ceiling. Another grunt. The lower part of the belt becoming a noose, cinching tight around the boy's thick, sportsman's neck.

Pinpointing the perfect moment to twist the proverbial knife in the boy's open psychic wounds, Pryce finally whispered, *"God will not forgive you."*

At that moment, the wall between the cells seemed to melt away under the witch-hunter's stoic gaze. With that barrier removed, Pryce could peer through the opening, as though staring down a long, dark tunnel and finding something most intriguing on the other side.

There was the boy, red cheeks puffed out, eyes bulging, spittle dangling from the corners of his lips. The belt cinched tighter and tighter, cutting into flesh as Ashton forced himself down, letting gravity play its part as well. Tears rolled slow from the boy's eyes.

The brown strap pressed tight against the boy's Adam's apple, robbing him of speech. However, there was nothing he could say, no regrets to express or prayers to offer, that would make a difference.

His legs went kick. Kick. Kick. A dark stain spread across the front of his pants. Then, another kick. His shirt was pulled up above his stomach as he twisted one way and another. His tanned abdomen and well-defined muscles gave the boy the appearance of a Greek demigod.

Useless, the witch-hunter thought, *all of it venal, pathetic, and so very useless.*

The boy's body shook. No more kicks followed. Seeing his work done, the witch-hunter bent down and reached for the scythe-like fingernail that'd grown oversized while lying on the floor of his cell.

First, he tested the heft and weight of the nail-scythe against his palm. Then, finding it acceptable, Pryce focused on what he could "see" in the cell next to his: the boy's face turning blue and purple. With the precision of a master sculpture turning raw clay to represent reality, Pryce raised the nail-scythe and slashed up, down, up, down, across, down, on and on. . .

He used the conjured weapon as a writing tool. He listened for the splitting of flesh in the other cell next door. The sounds of the word he wrote in the air before him manifested in the scratched and torn skin of the now-quite-dead boy's belly.

It wasn't until Pryce finished and a new cloud of his red-tinted mystical energy absorbed the nail-scythe, causing it to disappear from its current plane of existence, that Goodman Pryce spoke again and raised the alarm.

"Guard, I say, guards! There's. . . there's something wrong with the lad in the cell next to mine. Guards!"

Seconds later, they came running. And just as Pryce had used the ragged, bitten-off nail for the first part of his working, he'd soon use the dead boy's body as the conduit for his next spell. He knew that when the anguished, confused cries of the lawmen were raised and they stood about pulling at their hairs, rending their garments, and asking him, "Why? How could this happen? Who could do such a thing?" he'd have his answer ready.

"Who do you think did it? Just look, she's even signed her work."

* * *

"WITCH"

The word was unmistakable even when formed from jagged wounds across the boy's belly with his blood coagulating in a jammy mess at each puncture site. Now standing outside the holding cells, Pryce looked in at the word, his work. His gloves and hat were already returned to him, as well as his cutlass and blunderbuss—fetched from something called an "evidence locker."

The same lawmen, the ones who'd made the Sign of the Cross when they'd found the boy dead and desecrated and who'd offered prayers long before they'd thought to search for clues or seek answers to what happened, had proven easy enough to bend to the witch-hunter's side. All he'd had to do was offer a version of the truth, something to confirm the biases Pryce had sensed lurking within their hearts.

"My name is Nathaniel Pryce. I once lived in Fallen Church. I am a God-fearing man same as you. I am also a witch-hunter."

He did not even have to say "Don't laugh," as there was no one present who appeared to even consider the cracking of a smile.

"There's a witch in our town. Consorting with devils. She is intent on bringing ruin to our good, upstanding *Christian* home."

More nodding all around. Pryce hadn't even had to finish this pitch before a key turned in his cell door and he was granted his freedom.

"There is a great darkness coming," he told them all.

The witch-hunter's thoughts returned to the posters and placards he'd seen on the buildings downtown as he was driven to the station. Horrific painted interpretations of giant insects, painted garish colors, hovering above strange white and gray box-like contraptions with glowing glass windows at their centers. The images appeared so lifelike that Pryce had nearly asked his police escort if the pictures themselves were magical conjurations.

He'd thought better of it, of course. Even with his limited exposure to the time period, the witch-hunter had found the year 1999 was one nearly devoid of magic and miracles.

But not for much longer...

"THE Y2K BUG IS COMING"

That was what many of the broadsheets declared.

Different century, same doom-saying, Pryce had thought.

Still, there was something to those words, something Pryce believed with all his heart. *Every crisis is an opportunity.*

"I've seen the signs," he roared, feeling the town's men of justice bending further to his will with each uttered syllable. "They warn of pestilence at the dawn of the new millennium. The period of peace and prosperity you were no doubt told you were living in? You all have felt it slipping away, haven't you?"

A chorus of mumbled yeses and uh-huhs grew louder. Pryce turned to the man who'd brought him to the station. "Goodma. . . Officer Miller, did I hear something about reports of a bonfire? I would very much like to go there and speak with the young folk, our town's next generation, and warn them of the danger this witch presents for us all."

He caught sight of a redness in Miller's eyes, an encroaching crimson on the edges of the orbs. Pryce could see it in the eyes of every man and woman in the building, all of them fast becoming his acolytes. They gathered closer while the dead boy hung with his soiled pants and his fat dead tongue lolling out obscenely. They timed their breaths to match the witch-hunter's. They chanted slow and steady: "Witch. Bitch. Witch. Bitch."

Before, in Pryce's Fallen Church of long ago, more people were open to the idea of witches existing, but he'd still found himself alone, a solitary man doing the necessary work.

But here in this future, he didn't just have a few supporters. In this new world of Fallen Church, New Hampshire 1999, the witch-hunter had the beginnings of an army.

CHAPTER FIFTEEN

The window glass at the front of Nikki's house sprayed into their foyer as the first wave of angry, seemingly possessed high schoolers surged like a heavy wave against the building. Seeming to care little for their bodies, the teens punched and kicked at the windows. Others rammed their bodies against the front door. One after the other.

Inside, still reeling from the news of what'd apparently occurred at the police station, as delivered in breathless fashion by DiDi following a phone call from a fellow dancer who lived near the site, Josey stood frozen, watching the ongoing assault on the Farrs' home. Their front door buckled, hinges straining and then snapping, before it was pulled free from the frame. Already, ruddy, out-of-breath, and panting faces were thrust through the remnants of the windows, glittering glass shards decorating greasy, soot-streaked hair, appearing as diamonds amid the coal.

It reminded Josey of playing Resident Evil. Except there weren't zombies crawling and clawing at each other, all trying to be the first to get at Josey and the other women inside the house. They were her classmates. They were people she knew. Even if she didn't always like them and sometimes endured their cruelty while dreaming of vengeance, she didn't necessarily think of them as *evil*.

Sure there are some assholes. Folks like Ashton and his goons. But they don't. . . they don't deserve to die.

Don't they? Rebecca interjected, giving voice to her descendant's darker impulses.

Rebecca's question stung. It was the same question she'd turned over and over before the summoning, before the witch-hunter, before all the death and destruction. Josey had tried her damnedest not to think about it.

And it was exactly because the unspoken answer implied by her ancestor's intonation matched the same conclusion Josey had reached time and time again. In her lowest moments, she'd imagined her tormentors dead. Only the notion of escaping and leaving Fallen Church behind had kept those brutal impulses in check.

Josey knew she could escape, but she wasn't so sure about Nikki.

It seemed Linda Farr was on the witch's side. Grabbing a full bottle of Jack Daniels, one she'd likely squirreled away in some nook or cranny of her hoarder's paradise, Linda swung it with wild abandon, using it as a bludgeon, holding off the forward progress of the mob. "Get out of my house! Get the fuck out of my house!"

The weighted end of the liquor bottle thunked hard against the intruders' heads. Linda, proving more nimble than she appeared, dodged the grabbing hands of those who evaded her blows.

Nikki and DiDi stood by Josey's side. "You okay?" Nikki asked.

"I don't. . ." Josey couldn't figure out what the right answer should be.

"We gotta get out of here," DiDi said before Josey could find the answer.

Josey wanted to grab both of the sisters, pull them close, and scream questions at their faces. *"Where? Where the hell are we supposed to go? How do we stop this? What's going to happen to me. . . to us?"*

But she didn't have to do that. Because she still had a witch inside her head, a voice from their town's dark, shadowed past who was more than willing to give Josey the answers she sought.

Tell us how we stop the witch-hunter, Rebecca. What can we do?

"We need to go to the site of my execution," Rebecca spoke, using Josey as her conduit. *"The cycle must be completed. The execution site will have the necessary energy to power the spell needed. Pryce must return to my time and I must die."*

Peering out through her eyes, more passenger than driver, Josey watched DiDi take a step back, hearing her sister's friend speaking but also *not speaking*. It was the first time DiDi had directly witnessed the presence, and it seemed as big a shock and unsettling an experience for her as it had been for everyone else.

There was no time for anyone to process these strange revelations, however. Piles of old *Better Housekeeping* tipped over like dominoes, as Linda stumbled backward—out of the family's foyer and into their living room. Some time, during her drunken struggles with the mind-controlled teens, the liquor bottle had been smashed open at its bottom. The woodsy reek of bourbon wafted over Josey and the others as Mrs. Farr waved the busted bottle from side to side. Fire spread through the scattered debris, highlighting red droplets across the jagged peaks of broken glass.

"Go on! Get out of here!" Linda shouted, laughing between ragged breaths. Her adrenaline fading, the limitations of her not-well-kept body were catching up with her at last.

At first believing Mrs. Farr was referring to the trespassers, Josey and the Farr girls grabbed whatever they could and launched a counterattack, lobbing beer cans, ashtrays made of glass and porcelain, pristine kitchen gadgets still in their boxes, whatever they could get their hands on.

The sudden retaliatory bombardment provided enough of a shock to halt the invader's approach. However, the mindless fire had no such hesitation. Sweat dripped down Josey's forehead. Her clothes stuck to her body. Then, Linda grabbed Josey by her shirt and pulled the girl close, their foreheads almost touching.

"No," the older woman said, "I meant, you girls get. Get outta here. Take Nikki and DiDi. Get 'em outta this damned town like I shoulda done."

Josey wanted to protest. She wanted to insist that everything would be okay, that *everyone* would be okay. But when she glimpsed the fierce determination just below the surface of the other woman's watery, bloodshot eyes, all she could do was return a slight, acquiescing nod. With their contract sealed, Linda released Josey. The two women—the lost mother and the young witch—turned from each other, facing opposite directions. Linda moved first, letting loose a string of slurred expletives before barreling forward, slicing, slashing, and facing the attackers head-on.

Before Nikki or Didi could cry out to or follow their mother into the maelstrom, Josey grabbed each sister by their wrists. She let her momentum take over, giving her the extra strength needed to pull the Farr sisters to the back of their house. They passed through a cluttered kitchen, stinking of stale beer and spoiled food, the sink forever full of dishes.

Finally, they reached the back door. Josey let go of the other girls' hands and reached for the knob.

Her move was cut short by the ear-ringing *BOOM* of the witch-hunter's gun being fired. The explosion of pellets took out the inset window at the top of the door. A warning shot. The sulfurous stench of gunpowder offered a distinct note amid the fiery bouquets blooming across the house. And yet, it was this sudden attack that spurred Nikki and DiDi onward, giving them the push needed to move, to flee from their home. DiDi yanked the door open and waved her sister through.

"Josey! Come on!" DiDi cried, again playing the role of protector. However, Josey wasn't feeling much like being protected. She stared back across the inferno, witnessing Linda's arm pulled back the wrong way by one of her classmates. Pulled and pulled until it went *CRACK*. Josey decided she'd had just about enough of other people making sacrifices for her.

She thrust a hand back at DiDi and let loose a new discharge of crackling, blue-tinged energy. Her whole being tapped into powers beyond human comprehension. Serving as extra appendages, she let the mystical growths extend from her palms to embrace her friend's sister, all before shoving her out of the house and into the backyard beyond.

Her spell work finished, Josey returned to facing the inferno.

Nathaniel Pryce was there, waiting for her. He didn't make threats or offer anything new in the way of words. His face displayed the smirk she'd already come to loathe.

I know the perfect counter for that, she thought.

Indeed, Josey could already imagine Pryce's arrogant grin fading as she shook her head and turned from what seemed an inevitable confrontation. There would be no arcing streams of mystical energy here, no magical battle across a fiery landscape. Instead, she opened the back door again and ran into the darkness of the yard, ready to reunite with her friend.

"Not here, asshole," she whispered under her breath.

Now you've made him angry, Rebecca said inside of Josey's head. *Good*.

CHAPTER SIXTEEN

Francis Mundy hated the town of Fallen Church. He'd hated it for nearly all of his life, and after recently passing into middle age while remaining stuck living (if it could be called that) in the town, Mundy saw no end in sight to his hatred. It was easy to harbor such displeasure. After all, this was this same tiny town that'd seen him bullied, harassed, teased, and tormented as a child, even more so as a young adult. It wasn't just the people of Fallen Church who engaged in the ritualized torture of an aspiring artist, that most sensitive of souls who was called every pejorative and derogatory term under the sun. The town itself, the very physical space of it, seemed determined to keep Francis Mundy stuck, simmering in dislike.

How else to explain those poor road conditions— with potholes the size of small dogs— and the freak nor'easter blowing through one night during his senior year at Fallen Church High, the combo resorting in the storm-battered car accident that saw him walk away unscathed, but both his parents paralyzed. What else could he do but give up being a dreamer and become their caretaker instead?

And that's just what he'd done, giving up a scholarship to art school in New York, setting aside his escape plan. Pushing his dreams back and back and back. Of course, he had.

Instead of becoming one artist of many in the Big City, instead of finding others who he'd hoped were his people—dreamers whose visions extended beyond the limits of *their* small hometowns, Mundy settled for being Fallen Church's "Artist." Not a glamorous position, more matter-of-fact than anything else.

Taking community college classes, doing sign and poster commission work for Fallen Church businesses, designing walking tour graphics for the town's local landmarks—mostly involving him doing his best Rembrandt to capture images of the Fallen Church Witch and her execution. All of his generational cohort, such as it was, either moved from Fallen Church and never looked back, or remained the sort of people that Mundy wanted nothing to do with. They were to a man and woman, arrogant and ignorant in equal measure. Mundy had no clue how long he might've sleepwalked down that particular path.

Until, a chance encounter while ducking out for the donuts and coffee needed to fuel a flash of inspiration for a mural he wanted to paint on one side of his family home, caused great change in thirty-something Mundy's life. The school district's superintendent spotted the artist in line for coffee, homing in on him like a heat-seeking missile.

"Ever thought about teaching?" the man asked, smiling too wide, breathing too heavily.

Of course, Mundy *hadn't* thought of it. He hadn't been much in the way of long-term planning for a decade or more, seemingly resigned to his fate. But he also hadn't *not* thought of it. So he'd taken down some information from the school official, run through some more community college classes, and applied for the job of art teacher at Fallen Church High.

Returned to his old battlegrounds, back where he'd endured so much torment and torture but also experienced his greatest triumphs, Mundy found things somewhat different this time around.

For one, he'd soon realize that he was no longer alone, no longer the solitary outlier in a town of conformed masses. There were others. Kids—he realized he'd been just as much of a kid back in his would-be glory days—who all wanted a chance to express themselves or to show the world what they'd seen reflected back and back and back. With this new understanding came a new life's purpose. Mundy realized that even if *he* couldn't find a way out for himself, even if his destiny and that of his hometown were forever linked, then he could still strive to help others find *their* escape routes.

So each year, Mundy strove to find the outcasts, the outsiders, and those who thought beyond the limitations of the proverbial box. Through these new connections, he found friendship, mutual respect, and shared in dreams of building something that actually mattered. Some years, there was no one. More of the same from Fallen Church.

But other years? In other years, he'd find creative sparks lighting up the darkness, causing him to remember the twin joys of teaching and making art, as easy as spotting lightning bugs in the summer months.

The two girls in black and dark purples, the pair of them in leather and lace, with collared rings around their necks and so many piercings, their pen and ink sketches of future tattoos rendered with meticulous care on their hands and up their arms, they were the two latest lights that art teacher Mundy had picked out from the darkness. Josey and Nikki—their gothic clothing and put-upon morbid attitudes were not too far removed from Mundy's hippie past, his forced ideals of "sticking it to the Man"—were the end of the millennium's version of what he'd seen and been all those years before. Another decade, another cultural disguise. Naturally, he'd done what he could to encourage the both of them, displaying their work in class, getting special dispensation from the principal to show pieces in the front of the school, and even sliding art school brochures into Josey's locker. Both of them had promise, of course. But Josey? She was the one who seemed to have the spark—that magical something. Mundy was certain she'd change the world. Or at least be someone who got the hell out of Fallen Church.

Perhaps what he appreciated most about both girls was the way they'd lifted him up in response. Despite her protests to the contrary, Josey especially seemed fascinated by the history of Fallen Church, willing to learn more about where they'd come from and how they'd gotten to where they were. She was the one who found out about Mundy's past artistic triumphs. "I didn't know you were an artist-*artist*, Mr. Mundy. That's *sooooo* cool." No amount of practiced cynicism could mask the genuineness of the young woman's enthusiasm.

It made his heart beat half a beat faster. Eventually, he'd worked up the courage to share more of his past with the girls, giving them a look at his abandoned works, and talking to them about the things he'd planned to do before Fallen Church dug its claws into him.

"So why not do them now? Why not show the world what you can create?" Their questions made it all sound so simple.

And, in truth, he'd had no rebuttal, at least none that seemed capable of withstanding their withering, no-bullshit teenage appraisal. In addition, he'd quickly realized that continuing to abandon his dreams meant he'd give them an out, an excuse, a reason to give up *their* plans for *their* futures.

So that was how Mr. Mundy began work on a gallery showing of his art, a showcase to be presented in the town of Fallen Church. He'd converted part of his classroom into studio space reserved for him and his work alone.

And, of course, Josey and Nikki, his students, muses, and friends (though he'd hardly admit that aloud for professional reasons) ended up coming through for him one more time, bringing him the final piece of the puzzle earlier that Friday, arriving late for class and smelling of cigarettes and garbage.

"Here ya go, Mundy," Josey had said, shoving a handful of black-and-gray, shimmering VHS tape unwound from its casing into his hands. "Maybe you can use this for your show."

Before he could ask his follow-ups, the duo was off in a corner of the art room, sketching symbols that wouldn't look out of place on the sleeve of a heavy metal album or glimpsed by someone flipping through ancient library books dipped in dust and cobwebs. He'd left the girls to whatever they were planning, knowing that whatever it was, it would at least be interesting.

Besides, he liked the idea of a mystery. That's how he'd ended up "borrowing" equipment from Mr. White in the AV department and slipping Hoskins the janitor a couple of twenties to keep the side door unlocked on Friday evening so he could sneak back in and work on his exhibit and this new element—the element that would prove to be the centerpiece of the whole damned thing.

White and his AV club had recently purchased a

machine that could convert VHS content to "digital." It was all White could talk about in the teacher's lounge, though Mundy wondered how the digitized content and machinery might fare once that Y2K bug hit on January first *and* how it was that the school budget allowed for tech gadgets, but there was no money for extra colored pencils for his art students. Mundy kept both thoughts to himself, having learned long ago not to rock the boat when it came to how things were done in Fallen Church.

Whatever, he'd thought, *I'll get my money's worth at least.*

So it was that after hours of meticulously winding the tape back into the casing, inserting it into the marked slot and carefully following the instructions (with "Property of the AV Club Do Not Remove" stamped on the top) line by line that Mundy captured images from Josey's tape and made them a part of his own creation.

After spending more time running back and forth between his office and the deluxe printer in the teacher's lounge, he'd sat back and admired the posterized, printed-out images of oversized figures with slight VHS grain across their visages from the tape transfer. With that last-minute addition, Mundy was certain that next week would be the perfect time to finally share his exhibit and remind the people of Fallen Church that he was much more than some quiet, nervous-looking art teacher.

Then came the shouts and screams from down the

hallway, followed by the heavy-handed pounding on the door to the art room, with Josey, Nikki, and another young woman he recognized as Nikki's older sister—the one who now worked at the gentlemen's club on the outskirts of town, if what the football coaches said was true—all barging into the classroom, eyes darting this way and that, mouths curling into half-formed questions and renewed pleas for help.

All of it was overwhelming, incomprehensible. But everything slowed back down when Josey walked to the wall where an oversized blown-up image of a Barbie Doll dressed in crudely sewn black clothing and tied to a burning popsicle stake waited for her. She placed a hand on the image of fire.

She drew that hand back quickly as if she expected to be burned.

"Whaddaya know," she said, seemingly talking to herself. "Maybe this *is* where they killed you."

The two sisters also focused on the image of the burning witch doll. When Josey spoke again, two things became clear to Mundy. First: it wasn't Josey herself speaking. Second: whoever was speaking, seemed to share a kinship with that still image of the molded plastic figure transformed into 2D art.

"Wonderful work," she said. *"It's almost like you were there..."*

CHAPTER SEVENTEEN

"Can one of you get Mundy a glass of water?" Josey asked the Farr sisters. Her art teacher —the *only* teacher she liked in the whole school—looked as though he might fall over at any minute, and, based on the ritual that her ancestor had laid out for them, Josey figured their makeshift coven would need all the help they could get to finish the spell meant to banish Nathaniel Pryce the witchhunter back into the past, back to the moment of Rebecca's capture when he would become a part—a small part—of Fallen Church history before being forgotten forever.

Josey snapped her fingers in front of Mundy's face, trying to keep him focused on the here and now. *Snap.* "Mundy." *Snap.* "Hey, Mr. Mundy!" *Snap.* "Mundy! You with me?"

By the time she'd got his attention again, both sisters were approaching with glasses of water at the ready. Mundy shook his head at the glass offered by DiDi. "No, no," he said. "That's a cleaning jar."

Instead, he took the clean water cup from Nikki and drank from it slowly. In that moment of calm, Josey watched her teacher's Adam's apple bob up and down with each swallow.

When he finished, Mundy wiped his forearm across his mouth. Then, he got down to business, clearly attempting to play the role of the adult in the room.

"Hold on, hold on, first, what're you all even doing here? It's a Friday night. Shouldn't you be, I dunno, like out celebrating our win at the big game?" he asked, his tone half-jokey but also a little confused. "I mean, I assume we won."

"Pull up a chair, Mundy," Josey said. "We've got quite a story to tell."

She quickly noticed how her art teacher did no such thing and how his eyes widened and his bottom lip trembled. Nikki nudged Josey, making a quick head tilt to the side. That's when Josey looked down and found her hand curled, her fingers crooked and then straightened, undulating like waves. One of the wooden chairs scattered around the art room hovered above the floor, bobbing closer to them, like an unsteady-footed toddler.

"That's part of the story," Josey said with a shrug. The chair dropped, four legs clattering against the floor.

* * *

Moments later and after some panicked breathing as the seemingly impossible tale was absorbed and processed, Mundy painted symbols on the walls and windows of his classroom, re-creating figures from one of the "spell books" Josey and Nikki had hidden around the room, saving them to flip through whenever they got bored. Using the eyes of her descendant to review these New Age-y texts, Rebecca had vetted the symbols, pointing out which ones were valid and which ones were "codswoddle."

Josey couldn't help but wonder if it wasn't the use of terms like "codswoddle" that'd convinced Mundy of the validity of his pupils' story.

I'd say it was the magics you performed, her ancestor said, cutting right to the point from inside her head. *Now, let's review the ritual once again. I'm certain we don't have much time and we can't afford to get this wrong.*

Josey couldn't ignore the air of impatience heard behind Rebecca's words. Seeing as she was the only one hearing the words, Josey felt her levels of agitation rising in equal measure to her ancestor's. "I'm doing the goddamned best I can. . ."

"What's that, Joe?"

Nikki's question, the concerned look in her eyes, these were more than enough to break Josey's heart for the thousandth, maybe the millionth time, that evening. After all, it was Josey and her ancestor who'd pushed Nikki and her sister from their home, forcing them to leave it and all their belongings to burn.

Leaving their mother in the clutches of the witch-hunter and his brainwashed army.

And still, there was Nikki. Asking Josey if *she* was all right, or if she was *okay*. It didn't seem fair as far as Josey could tell. She wanted to say something to her friend, offer apologies, maybe some heartfelt reassurances of her own. But before she could, Nikki reached across and held her hand.

Josey was sure Nikki would squeeze it, the way she had earlier in the evening. A quick, tight squeeze to remind her of their bond of friendship.

So it surprised the hell out of Josey when Nikki took her hand and brought the knuckles up to her mouth. Lips parted slightly, the girl Josey spent almost all her time with, the girl who helped her forget the teasing and mockery and complete and utter dismissal of everything she was, everything she wanted to be, by their classmates and neighbors and even family members, kissed that hand she held. Soft, gentle pressure against the thin skin of Josey's knuckles sent an electric shock sensation through her body.

Whatever Josey wanted to say in reply, it went right out the window. Instead, she brought her hand, the one freshly kissed by her best friend (and now *possibly more*), to her face. She laid that hand against her cheek like a lovelorn lady on the cover of one of the trashy romance novels her mom kept hidden around the house. Doing so, she smelled Nikki's peppermint hand cream and wanted the taste of it on her tongue.

"That was nice," she said.

"Yeah?" Nikki asked with a growing smile to match.

Josey could only nod. The other words she wanted to say just weren't ready to be said yet.

"I've been going through the spell with DiDi," Nikki said. "You're sure this is Rebecca's execution spot? Because if it's not. . . if it's actually where you went on your field trip. . ."

* * *

It wasn't the first time that question had come up. Fleeing from their second burning home of the evening, Josey had thought she was taking her rag-tag group of witch-hunter resistance to the spot she'd visited on that infamous field trip in middle school. After all, that was the place they were told that Rebecca Wesley had been killed, where the veil separating past and present was first severed, and where Josey had glimpsed her ancestor's grim fate.

They'd elected to travel by foot, after glimpsing the ransacking of Nikki's car by riotous youths in front of her burning home. They'd kept to the shadows, following hidden pathways between houses in the connecting, overlapping neighborhoods of Fallen Church. Fleeing from the broken glass smashing against asphalt, and from the polluted fire stench of burning houses that seemed to chase them, the three young women and one young woman's detached spirit unmoored from the past were like children engaging in a life-or-death game of freeze-tag or hide-and-seek.

But when Josey tried to move them in the direction of the reenactment site, her raised foot seemed to freeze mid-stride. A dull ache rose from her leg and up through her body to her head. *That's not where I'll be killed,* her ancestor said from inside Josey's head.

Well, where then?

Do you trust me? Rebecca asked.

Josey was slower to answer. After all, she'd seen the violence that the witch-hunter was capable of. Two homes destroyed, each burned to the ground moments after Josey had occupied them. People injured, dead. Including, quite likely, a loved one of someone she cared very deeply for. But not once in all the chaos of the night had she sensed any sadness, any regret, anything coming close to sympathy or pity for those people and places upon which the witch-hunter had left his mark, coming from her ancestor. Worse still, she'd found herself hard-pressed to conjure those same emotions inside herself. The dark emotionless void inside went beyond feigned indifference and play-acted cynicism. It was a sub-zero temperature drop deep in the pit of her stomach.

Do you trust me? There was Rebecca again. Rebecca the Fallen Church Witch. Trained and instructed in the dark arts by Nathaniel Pryce and then betrayed by him. *Of course, she'd want revenge. Of course, she'd want him stopped.*

But instead of looking inward, instead of

confronting her ancestor in the shared strange and
nebulous dreamscape that'd become commonplace for
her in almost no time at all, Josey returned her attention to her friend's ethereally beautiful face. There, she
found a look of trust, the other girl's features hopeful
—not for abstract ideas like the future, but *for* Josey
herself.

Nikki believed in her and in seeing that Josey had
felt the final decision being made for her. If *Nikki* could
believe in her, then she would believe in *herself*. She'd
open herself to trusting the voice within.

With conditions, of course.

I will, she said to the ghost in her head, *but you have
to promise me you'll do whatever it takes to keep my friend
safe.*

Having secured that concession, Josey had allowed
Rebecca to take over. Her body remote-controlled
across time, she'd found herself moving faster and
faster. The Farr sisters struggled to keep up. As she
moved, Josey heard place names familiar and not-so-
familiar buzzing around in her head spoken aloud in
the Old World dialect of her ancestor. The path they
blazed seemed somewhat familiar, but all she'd had
time to do was let her body go with the flow. It wasn't
until she heard her ancestor whisper, *Here. Here's the
spot of execution,* that Josey recognized where she and
the other two living young women had been led.

"The school?" Nikki asked, beating Josey to the
punch.

Josey had shrugged. Then, she'd noticed the lights

on in the art room and a plan leaped from her skull fully formed, just waiting to be put into action.

* * *

Soon, all that remained was the waiting. And luckily (or perhaps unluckily) enough, that period didn't last long at all. The next stage of the now townwide conflict kicked off with the revving of engines, the howl of police and fire-truck sirens, cacophonous voices in mumbling prayer—spouting generic Bible verses, and all growing louder and louder in volume. DiDi parted the blinds, the plastic snapping under her fingers, and peered out to the front of the school. She turned away quickly.

"It's not just your classmates anymore," she said. "Looks like that bastard's brought the whole damn town over to his side."

"So, it's the same as it ever was," Rebecca said, speaking through Josey.

A loose brick crashed through the window, a clichéd punctuation to a most bizarre call to arms. Glass shards cut at Didi's back, tearing chunks from her legs. She stumbled forward, crying in pain with each step. Nikki ran to her sister, offering her a shoulder to lean against. Soon, the sisters limped toward a nearby chair.

But before they'd made it all the way there, a pained cry rose up from outside of the building, the sound of which immediately had the sisters turned around and heading back the way they'd come.

"Help! Oh God! Help me!"

It was their mother, Linda, calling out in what sounded like unnatural, incomprehensible pain.

Even as the sisters beelined to the broken window, seemingly intent on climbing through the jagged opening and joining their mother, Josey and Mundy stepped forth, blocking their path. Josey glanced at her hands and noticed them already glowing with the same mystical energy whose creation she'd taken to so easily, so naturally. This light, created through her connection to forces both divine and demonic, reflected off her best friend's features. When she looked up, Josey found Nikki's expression a grim portrait of fear. Not only was her fear directed to the dangers waiting for them outside their school, but a fraction of it was pointed to Josey herself.

Seeing this reaction, Josey closed her eyes, willing the power back inside. Out of sight, if not out of mind.

When she opened her eyes, the energy was gone, but the standoff continued.

Linda's howling and animalistic mewling had not stopped. However, the rest of the witch-hunter's mob had fallen silent.

"Please," Josey said to the sisters, "we can't go out there. Not now. If we do we'll all be dead."

Outside, another shrill cry from Linda, "Help meeeeeee—" was suddenly cut off. All four individuals holed up in the art room now rushed to the busted-out window. Mundy yanked on the thin polyester cord, raising the broken blinds. They dangled over the frame like a giant animal's rib cage displayed as a hunting trophy. Through the hole left by shattered glass, they had a clear view of the gathered masses.

The entire population of Fallen Church was there, just as DiDi had suggested. Josey's stomach ached and her mouth went dry at the sight. So many faces, people she'd seen every day in class, in her neighborhood, and even in her home.

Because there was her mom and dad and brother too. Her brother was still in his band uniform, since all of his other clothes had burned to ash in that first devastating fire. The three held hands, a united front, like all the others who'd gathered there. United in opposition to Josey. All eyes were directed in rapt, worshipful attendance to the witch-hunter as his thick-soled boot ground down on the neck of the first accused—Nikki and Didi's drunken, hoarder mother.

CHAPTER EIGHTEEN

Goodman Pryce could speak with the voice of a practiced hellfire-and-brimstone preacher. He spoke that way when he intended his speech to be as close to the Word of God as many of the dim-witted peasants and habitual sinners with which he'd found himself surrounded—no matter the time period—would ever hope to reach. Of course, it was all an illusion, an act, a put-upon, and a performance.

That was one of the first lessons he'd taken from his true masters, those otherworldly instructors in the black arts, beings who dwelled in the darkness of the Earth, their kingdom a place of shadows.

If the performance is strong enough, you can get away with all kinds of evil in the name of their Lord God.

"Good people of Fallen Church, the woman before you stands accused of consorting with witches, giving succor and shelter to a witch and her coven."

Beneath his heel, the woman—a nasty and violent piece of work—struggled and squirmed, trying to free herself. Spittle flecked from her lips and the few gasping breaths Pryce allowed her were heavy with alcohol fumes.

"Do you confess?" he asked, his eyes piercing downward as though he could break into the woman's skull and scoop out the answer.

But there was no confession, no admission of guilt, forthcoming. Only howling, wordless and unceasing. Utterly undignified. Exactly as the witch-hunter expected. Exactly as he'd hoped for.

"Mama! Mama! We're sorry! Mama! We're trying to..."

The cries came from the open window of the so-called school where the witch and her makeshift coven had sought shelter. Pryce didn't hear the witch, nor did he hear the witch's descendant, the girl Josephine. Perhaps if he'd heard one voice from that family, the only family in Fallen Church that truly mattered to him, then he might have taken pause. He might have given his captive to the mob, allowing them to rend her limb from limb, so that her flesh and blood would be embedded under their fingernails.

But the witches of past and present remained silent.

Cowards.

Knowing more work was needed, more fuel required to light the fire under the townsfolk of Fallen Church and make them willing participants in the acts of death and destruction to come, Pryce understood a push was needed.

He lifted his foot off the woman's neck.

She choked and coughed, phlegm and spittle fountaining from her mouth, then drooling down her ruddy cheeks. At last, she caught her breath and her hoarse cries were like long-nailed fingers scratching at the minds of everyone present.

"Do. . . do whatever you want with me. Just. . . just leave *my* girls alone. . ."

"Tell us, do you consort with witches and the prince of darkness? Have you signed your wicked name in the Devil's black book?"

While he put on his performance for the gathered masses, Pryce allowed the mystical energies stored inside his body to flow outward through his glove-covered hands. Another bit of misdirection, it wasn't long until a dark shadow fell across the captured woman. Black and deep blues, enough like the abyss to hide the woman's face from all except Goodman Pryce.

"I don't know what you're talking about!" the woman shouted, sounding like a vagrant interrupted in the midst an alcohol stupor. Pryce supposed she wasn't that far off from such a label.

"If they are suspected of witchcraft and related sins, their body shall be crushed between boulders and large rocks until they are deceased."

All it took was a head tilt upward for the witch-hunter to draw his victim's and everyone else's attention skyward. There they found the large, heavy object he'd lifted off the ground with his powers, while they were all distracted by his words. In place of boulders and rocks, Pryce had been forced to adapt, getting more creative in the ways he carried out this execution.

The blue and white blinking lights of the "police car" glittered in the chill night sky.

Here is your judgment, he thought.

He chose to keep those words to himself. The most cruel and wicked parts of what remained of his soul wanted, *no, needed,* the woman to die confused, uncertain, and lost. That would be a pain far more insidious than what came next.

He brought his hands together, folding them as if in reverent prayer. And then, the vehicle crashed down onto the woman's prone form. Metal screaming, the ground shaking, the impact coughing up dirt and the remnants of dead grass. The vehicle fell with a force greater than one might expect.

That extra power was the witch-hunter's doing. Baiting the trap, making sure the next steps were followed as he'd envisioned. He applied more force, knowing the woman's death was an essential ingredient and one that could not be forsaken.

First, the woman's bodily destruction. Her limbs were severed. Her blood pooled onto the grass, mingling with the gasoline leaking from the ruined vehicle. If Pryce were to lift the heavy conveyance from the woman's ruined form, everyone in attendance would see her pulped and squashed. An insect destroyed under his boot heel.

Then, he heard the report of one of the peace officer's guns. The weapon discharged from inside the school. Again, it fired. Then, again. And again.

Unlike his blunderbuss, these new weapons required no waiting, no time required to reload after every blast.

The remaining glass in the broken window caught the glare of the artificial lights shining on the school. Then, the remaining shards burst loose from the frame as the thin, bleeding body of a man—a man who must have sided with the witch's coven—was flung back, accompanied by another report from the gun of the future as wielded by one of Pryce's newfound followers.

The bearded man was dead already. Dead, as he fell across the open window. His arms flung out and blood sprayed from his back. As if time slowed to a crawl, the blood spray appeared as a red-tinged angel's wings.

When the echo of gunfire receded, Pryce picked out fresh screams from the girls inside the school, the new coven in clear fear for their lives. Their terrified cries were sweet music to his ears. Then, another voice rose above the screams. A woman's voice, that of the acolyte he'd armed and sent into the building because she had a key and knew the layout, sang in reverent ecstasy, saying, "Praise the Lord."

Goodman Pryce couldn't help but agree. *His* Lord was indeed worthy of praise. He made the sign of the reverse cross and whispered a prayer.

"Hail Satan."

CHAPTER NINETEEN

Given the earlier events of the evening, Josey should have guessed that her history teacher might try to kill her. Certainly, there was already the bad blood between them—what with the frequent punishments, the trips to the dumpster at the side of the school and to the principal's and guidance counselor's offices, or the way Ms. Roberts allowed the other students to gang up on Josey only to turn around and act as if it were all the weird goth girl's fault. Josey knew the history teacher didn't *like* her and at worst maybe the woman imagined her no longer existing, but only in the abstract. And certainly, Josey had reciprocated that notion. But never seriously. More the occasional venting of frustrations.

However, Mr. Mundy's bullet-riddled body hanging half in and half out of the art room window, with his head tilted back so his dead eyes stared at the smashed police car under which her friend's mother lay smashed and smeared, served as a reminder to Josey that the stakes were quite literally life and death.

* * *

Josey hadn't even had time to process the violent, Grand Guignol-style execution of her best friend's mother at the hands of Goodman Pryce. Even as that police car slammed down with excessive force and velocity and decimated the poor woman's body, Josey and the others in the art room had their viewing of the carnage interrupted. The door slammed open and someone stepped in from the hallway.

Ms. Roberts held a handgun in front of her like a divining rod. Both hands wrapped tight around the weapon—part of Fallen Church P.D.'s standard carry. Both of the history teacher's arms shook as she moved forward. As though the weapon itself were leading her onward, pulling her. However, she'd still maintained enough control to tighten her trigger finger and fire.

The first shot went wide. The bullet slammed into the wall beside one of the sigils the girls had carefully painted moments before.

We must not let her ruin the ritual!

Josey couldn't believe the words she heard from her ancestor. No sadness, no fear for the safety of the others, no sympathy whatsoever. If she'd had more time, more of her wits about her, Josey might have said something—*thought something*—back into the past, rejecting Rebecca's way of thinking. But by the time the words would have come, Ms. Roberts had pulled the trigger again.

Josey felt hands on her back moments prior to that

second firing. The hands belonged to Mr. Mundy. He pushed her to the ground, away from the window. At the same time, Nikki and DiDi must've dove to the floor, throwing themselves to the opposite side of the window. The art teacher might've had some command to share or a word of warning for the young women. Something like "Run!" or "Hide!" or "Go! Live! Leave!" Something, anything.

But whatever those words would've been, got blown right out of him as more bullets slammed into his chest and made their bloody, gory exit out his back. Like a marionette with tangled strings, limbs crossed and crisscrossed as the bullets from the history teacher's gun slammed into him and drove him through the window.

The gunfire echoed in Josey's ears and the stench of the weapon's discharge made her gag. She'd glanced to the side and found the Farr sisters crab-walking toward a hiding place, trying to shelter behind some turned-over desks and an art supply cart Mr. Mundy used to bring paint and brushes, chalk and charcoal, and more to each student's desk.

Ms. Roberts remained standing stock still, arms outstretched and gun in hand. Unloading more bullets into Mr. Mundy's very dead body. "Witch bastard. Witch bastard. Witch bastard. . ." she'd said, muttering a variation of what had become, for Josey, a very familiar tune indeed.

She must be stopped. There was Rebecca again. Speaking to her descendant with a confidence that could only come from *not* being the one in immediate danger. Josey couldn't stop herself from having that exact thought.

The wave of psychic backlash across the centuries from past to present was enough to knock Josey flat, causing her to black out for a moment. Her eyelids fluttered. The last thing she heard before losing consciousness was her ancestor's voice, her formerly soft tones turned to screeching.

HAVE YOU FORGOTTEN THAT I AM THE ONE WHO'S SUPPOSED TO DIE? ALL OF THIS. . . EVERY PART OF THIS RITUAL. . . IT'S INTENDED TO KEEP YOUR PRESENT, MY FUTURE, THE WAY IT'S ALWAYS BEEN. ONE DEAD WITCH, ONE FORGOTTEN WITCH-HUNTER! WHAT DO YOU KNOW OF SACRI-FICE. . . WHAT DO YOU KNOW OF LOVE?

* * *

As if freshly spoken, Rebecca's words echoed in Josey's ears. Pressing her back to one of the walls, Josey wiped at her eyes, trying to clear away the gunk gumming up her vision. Her hands came away red and sticky with blood, the top she wore was stained crimson with bloody tears. She moved her head this way and that, trying to get her bearings.

There was the window. Still broken.

With Mr. Mundy draped across the frame. Still dead.

Nikki was crawling toward her. But Josey

couldn't ignore the rest of the scene and do what she wanted more than anything—to focus entirely on the girl she cared for, the girl she was pretty sure she loved.

What do you know of love?

The sounds of struggle pulled Josey's attention away from her ancestor's voice.

There were still two others in the art room, two that hadn't been accounted for yet.

DiDi fought the history teacher. The middle-aged schoolmarm and the young, but world-wearied, stripper were punching, biting, slapping, and kicking at each other. The gun had been kicked away, its black handle sticking out from under one of the tables. With the weapon removed from the equation, the odds were evened, even favoring DiDi.

Yet when Josey saw Ms. Roberts sink her teeth into the tanned flesh of the younger woman's shoulder, shaking her head back and forth like a rabid dog, and then witnessed DiDi hauling back and punching the older woman full force in the face, smashing the teacher's nose to blood-soaked pieces, she could tell that something was very wrong. Roberts fought with the fierceness of a zealot, like she'd found a Holy Crusade worth waging.

But DiDi's face, with a look of fear similar to the one Josey had seen Nikki wearing, did not suggest that she wished to engage in the balletic exchange of violence playing out in the art room.

"Stop!" DiDi managed to choke out, spitting

chipped and broken fragments of teeth past busted, bleeding lips smeared into a too-wide smile shape.

Only she wasn't speaking to her attacker. Her eyes were on Josey.

At first, Josey didn't understand why.

Not until Nikki was beside her, grabbing at her friend. For a split second, Josey thought the other girl was going to take her face in her hands and pull it in for a kiss. But Josey didn't want that, not yet. There were still words that she wanted to say first, her own magic words—or at least words that felt magical to her.

Those words—the idea of sharing *those* words—disappeared like so much smoke, when Nikki's hands dropped and grabbed at Josey's. Only then, when Josey saw her friend's appendages engulfed in the unnatural glowing blue energy radiating out from her without even knowing she was making it, and after she heard Nikki scream as the unchecked supernatural power rippled up her arms, did Josey understand what'd happened while she was unconscious.

She was the one, using her witch's powers, to control DiDi and force her to fight their history teacher—a woman who was herself a pawn under the witch-hunter's control.

Don't stop. Don't let her stop you. There was Rebecca again, commanding her descendant to forsake everyone else and focus only on their time-spanning mission.

Josey felt torn in two, at least from the inside. Part

of her in the present, part of her thrust back to that woodland clearing where her witchy ancestor lay atop dead leaves, eyes rolled back white, in a trance-like state.

She felt her hands, still aglow with witchy energy and infernal power, the light produced growing lighter and lighter, moving toward a bright, white-hot radiance. She heard the sharp hissing sizzle, the sound cutting through Nikki's cries of pain. In the present, she watched her friend's hands redden and blister, unable to handle the power coursing out of Josey.

In the past, Josey saw her ancestor moving. Hand on her belly, massaging the place where her infant child had grown—the child Rebecca would never see again. That same child who'd eventually start the Wesley line anew, the descendants producing male heir after male heir. Until Josey.

Until the girl who'd inherit the witch's power.

In the present, DiDi and Ms. Roberts were on the floor, bleeding, beaten, and bruised. But still fighting like wild cats, each scrambling to reach the gun.

And in the past? Pushing aside whatever commands Rebecca tried placing in her mind, Josey focused on the physical form of her ancestor. She saw the young woman's lips moving, watched them forming a name. She focused, pushing away all distractions past and present and even those from the future. Silencing the interweaving timelines around her, she could finally pick out the name on Rebecca's lips.

And there it was:

"Nathaniel."

Then, she understood. With that understanding came a realization that a part of her had perhaps known the whole while. After all, hadn't there been something in the eyes and chin, the slope of the ears of the witch-hunter that'd seemed strangely familiar to her? The monstrous eyes and lips were a distraction from his more subtler traits. Certainly there was some inflection in his speech that stirred up feelings of déjà vu?

It was him. Goodman Pryce, the witch-hunter, was the father of your child. He's my ancestor too. You and him both.

CHAPTER TWENTY

The witch's silence—in both past and present —served as confirmation enough. And with that confirmation, that the witch-hunter was the father of Rebecca Wesley's child, Josey found she'd regained control of her body and her burgeoning powers. She recalled the mystical energy holding Nikki, releasing the girl to pull her wounded hands against her body and rock back and forth on the floor.

Before Josey could offer apologies, she knew what message she had to send back through the fog of time.

I love her, yes. Yes, I do. I love her. And I don't think she'll betray me. Not the way Pryce betrayed you.

But you can't be sure! There was Rebecca, the *first* witch of Fallen Church—though not the first mortal in the village to dabble in black magic—finding her voice again.

It's never about being sure though, Josey shared across time. *It's about believing. Believing there's still something good. Giving yourself over to that belief.*

Josey opened her eyes and found Nikki standing

before her, holding out her injured hands, as if presenting them for inspection. The small smile on the other girl's face, the way she reached across with one of those injured hands and brushed strands of Josey's dark hair away, told Fallen Church's newest witch that her words were not only heard and felt by her ancestor but had also reached the other survivors in the art room.

Josey took Nikki's hands and brought them to her mouth, holding them just shy of her lips.

A gasp sounded across the room, drawing the attention of both girls. DiDi was on the floor. She seemed free, at last, of supernatural manipulation, in control of her body once more. However, she wasn't clear of the danger just yet.

Ms. Roberts had the gun.

"DiDi!" Nikki cried out and made a move toward her sister.

This time, Josey wouldn't use her powers or physical action to stop her friend. She opted to rely on her words and trusted that her friend would still be willing to listen.

"Wait," she said.

There was hesitation. And it was enough to keep Nikki at her side. This same hesitation was mirrored by their history teacher keeping her finger off the trigger and holding the barrel down, away from DiDi.

"I heard a voice inside my head. We all did. The Man. The Hunter. Told me to kill you. Told me you were all witches."

"Ms. Roberts," Josey started, "I'm sorry. I'm sorry for everything..."

"He's calling again. Singing his sweet little song. But I know what that song is now. It's the Devil's song..."

Later, Josey might try to convince herself that Rebecca had, once again, reached forward from the past to stop her descendant from intervening. But Josey would know the truth, a truth she'd have to live with for the rest of her life: it was *her* choice and her choice alone to keep her hands by her side, her powers in check.

She refrained long enough for Ms. Roberts to take the gun and turn it on herself. Barrel under her chin, trigger pulled, brains splattered against the door. Like a deflated balloon, her body slithered to the ground, a hissing accompanying her fall.

After DiDi scrambled back, away from the dead body, joining the other young women, the trio embraced. They worked together to ensure each member of the party stood on their own two feet despite the terrible weight of all that'd transpired that evening.

Despite the immediate danger ending, they couldn't miss the sounds of marching feet, of murmuring voices that repeated the witch-hunter's adopted chorus. "Witch bitch, witch bitch, witch bitch..."

It seemed the witch-hunter was enacting his endgame.

Josey surveyed the room, taking in the damaged walls riddled with stray bullet holes, the broken window, and the bloodied bodies of their teachers. However, the painted symbols were still intact, the salt circle was still more or less undisturbed, and the Rebecca-vetted spell book pages were ready for recitation.

She knew what came next, as sure as she'd known anything in her life. And, just as confessing her love for Nikki after all those years of longing, that surety felt good. It demanded action.

Lucky for Josey, the Farr sisters looked to her for answers. And she had them to share.

"Time for us witch bitches to send this asshole back to the dusty past where he belongs."

As words were spoken, the art room, the school, and the entire town of Fallen Church plunged into the darkness.

CHAPTER TWENTY-ONE

Goodman Pryce cursed himself for trusting a woman, even one like the so-called teacher of history who'd expressed as much faith as he might have hoped for among his throng of followers. Controlling her until the moment when the new witch, Rebecca's descendant and, yes, his as well, had unleashed a surge of power, freeing the crone from the witch-hunter's control. Freeing her long enough for the damage to be done.

Look what she did. Killed herself. Weak, stupid woman. Not a hunter. Not like me.

Pryce was thankful that he'd made backup plans. Before they'd made it to the school grounds, he'd spoken to the townsfolk under his control.

They'd stared at him in slack-jawed wonder. Their dull faces made the witch-hunter shudder, as he considered what fate might lie ahead for himself and the people *his* Fallen Church if these simple sinners were to be their legacy.

"Tell me the prophecies," he'd commanded. "Tell

me what will happen at the turn of the millennium. This Y. . . 2. . . K."

The answer, from someone with an officious face and a tailored suit to match, came in a clipped and canned fashion as if the man spoke by reciting a spell, the same as the witches no doubt hoped to do inside the school building.

"Don't worry about that, pal. We've been running tests. Making sure all our systems operate the way they're supposed to, even when the clocks change at midnight. The worst thing that might happen is rolling blackouts. But nothing permanent."

Pryce seized on the words, finding a way to direct them toward his ends.

"Blackout," he said. "So we could stop this. . . power? Take away the lights?"

"Yeah, but, we won't have to. . ."

"Do it." Pryce's command provided no opportunity for objection or protest. He stood with hands on hips, sneer on face, waiting until some of the men broke away from the crowd, setting themselves up to complete the witch-hunter's special mission.

Later, when Pryce ordered his followers to break into the school and finish the work the now-dead history teacher had started, he'd watched wide-eyed as the false lights blinked quickly—once, twice—and then went out. Not just in the school, but in the tall, arched poles holding their false suns. In the blink of an eye, they no longer illuminated the paths. The houses and storefronts and every building nearby, all went black.

"Let there be darkness," he said with an amused chuckle, enjoying the twist on that all-too-common Biblical command.

The witch-hunter's followers acted as his vanguard, smashing at the glass and steel façade of the school building. Many were already cut, burned, and bleeding from previous encounters. All of them were worn-down, bone-tired. The exhaustion on their faces reminded Pryce of the people living back in his Fallen Church. Fighting the land, the elements, each other, everyone doing everything they could to survive.

It was easy to manipulate people that worn and weary, desperate for answers and seeking someone to blame even if they hadn't quite known that yet. *Perhaps this Fallen Church is not so different than the one I left behind.*

He pointed at posters and glass cases containing golden statuary, signaling to his followers that these idols and heathenistic illuminated manuscripts were to be destroyed. Coming across a library, its stocked shelves full of books without a Bible among their number, Pryce encouraged others in his flock to set those tomes aflame. The sound of burning paper and the pop of melted binding glue was music to the witch-hunter's ears.

However, his nose picked up something beyond

ink-scented smoke. He breathed in deeply, filling his lungs with the scent of witch.

He didn't have to search for long. Not Nathaniel Pryce the witch-hunter, would-be hero of Fallen Church. He knew his hunt would soon end.

And yet...

Something nibbled at Pryce's thoughts. Its persistence reminding him of a barnyard cat toying with a captured mouse. *How he hated those whiskered beasts!*

With that vague sense of danger in mind, Pryce commanded his followers to go ahead. He'd let violence serve as angel's trumpets announcing his arrival to the coven.

CHAPTER TWENTY-TWO

Nikki struck her lighter, and its flame flickered, before burning steady. Her thumb pressed the red plastic fork, ensuring the flame and its light both stayed alive. With her other hand, she shoved a copy of the spell into Josey's hands. She kept a copy for herself. There was a third copy, one she tried to give to her sister.

But DiDi, her face yellowing and purpling with fresh bruises, her eyes visible through puffy slits care of the pummeling she'd received, refused. Instead, she gestured, first to the door, already buckling under the strain of attackers hellbent on breaking into the art room, and then to the open window, with room for trespassers left despite the presence of Mundy's corpse. DiDi had the gun and had also broken off part of a painter's easel, crafting a crude cudgel from it, paint-splattered and notched up and down its length.

"Whatever's going on there, you don't need me for that. I'm gonna do what Mama would've wanted, try and keep you safe and outta trouble," she said.

Josey found herself blinking away tears, and it wasn't even her family member who was speaking. When she looked at Nikki, her friend was wiping her eyes with the spell book pages, while keeping the lighter's flame going in her other hand.

"Thank you," Josey said to DiDi.

Following her statement, the thick wooden door finally buckled under the pressure, sending tan-colored splinters of treated wood flying around the art space.

DiDi laughed. "Don't thank me yet," she told her sister's friend. "Once I'm gone, you're the one who's gonna have to look after her next."

Nikki's light flickered, blinking out for a second. She winced before the flint was struck and the flame reappeared.

"You okay?" Josey asked.

Nikki nodded. "It's only a little pain," she said. "We've had worse."

"*He's coming*," Rebecca spoke through Josey.

In unison, Josey, Nikki, and even DiDi replied. "We *know!*"

The first wave of intruders trampled across the broken door. DiDi pulled the trigger, testing the gun for more bullets, seeing what might remain in its clip.

Fate smiled down on her. The white and gold-embroidered top of a band uniform worn by the first person through the doorway blossomed red, like she'd given the attacker a boutonniere for prom.

Glimpsing this from the corner of her eye, Josey

had no time to see if the person shot had been her baby brother. There was no time left, no time to save individuals one by one. She knew the spell-working that she had to do. A true spell. Josey and Nikki would perform part of the ceremony on one end, while Rebecca did her thing in the past.

Josey began by invoking the necessary goddesses. "Hecate, Diana, Lilith, Persephone, hear the pleas of your servants. . ."

Standing in the salt circle, close enough so their heads touched, Josey and Nikki read through their portion of the ritual, performing the necessary hand gestures and providing offerings via objects found in their pockets or scavenged from the classroom.

". . . sands of time, ascend the hourglass confines. . ."

DiDi's grunts and screams, the click of her now-emptied clip, and the smack of hot metal and cold, paint-splattered wood against the flesh of her attackers covered the sounds of the ritual.

Josey caught Nikki's eyes drifting and saw the tiny flame quivering. She cleared her throat, trying to draw her friend's attention back, trying not to interrupt the ceremony, but also wanting to get her message across.

"You can go if you want to. . . I can finish this," she whispered

None of that was necessary, however. After the ordinary citizens of Fallen Church, all of them caught up in the frenzied excitement of the witch-hunter's commandments, fell or retreated under DiDi's assault, the rapid-fire *pop-pop-pop* of multiple handguns being fired at once, marked the arrival of the Fallen Church police department.

DiDi's last words came as a defiant snort and a scream of "Pigs!"

Nikki fell to her knees. The lighter slipped from her grasp and all returned to darkness with flickering after-images.

Josey wanted to join her friend on the floor. She wished she could pull the other girl into an embrace that'd take them both to the grave.

But she couldn't do it. She knew that. The town of Fallen Church might not have always loved her. But it was the only home she'd known. In this way, Josey felt like she finally understood why her ancestor chose to hide in the woods on the outskirts of her village, rather than running away and finding somewhere new to start her life again.

Like her ancestor, Josey knew she'd rather fight and fix the resulting problems later than surrender and let her immediate problems win.

So she'd remained standing, holding the spell book pages close to her eyes and trying her damnedest to read them in the dark. She didn't turn around when the gasping, breathy croaks of the police officers-turned-deputy-witch-hunters commanded her to "Put her hands up!" or "Turn around!" or "Get on the ground!"

One officer even went so far as to tell Josey, "Don't make me hurt you."

That last line was the equivalent of a mosquito's whine on the last day of summer. In response, Josey made a quick, flippant gesture with her free hand, borrowing a portion of the power she was using to open a portal across space-time. She flung a spectral ball of conjured light back in the face of the offending officer.

With a flash and bang, the ball exploding in the face of the lawman cast a white light across the room. Almost *too* white, *too* bright.

"Enough!"

There he was. It was only at the sound of *his* voice that Josey finally turned from her spell work.

Pryce regarded her with the cruel smile, one that had grown so familiar to her. His bulbous eyes were bloodshot, while his hands glowed red. He opened one hand like someone's father playing catch. Except there was no seamed, dust-covered baseball released from his palm, but rather more crimson-tinged lightning, traveling sideways across the room, hitting the paper in Josey's hand and setting the spell ablaze.

"You *don't* win," Pryce said; and Josey was uncertain if he spoke to her or to Rebecca back in the past, a past she found was coming into sharper and sharper focus. "I've seen this future and there are no witches here. *I win.*"

But Josey wouldn't let that stop her. She continued chanting, performing as much of the ritual as she could remember. Her fingers ran through Nikki's hair as the girl she loved pressed her body against the leg of the new witch from Fallen Church. Nikki's lips moved in time with Josey's, no sound emerging but the effort, *some effort* was made.

When Pryce threw out another bolt of energy aimed at Nikki's head, Josey countered, waving her arms, producing a blue-tinged force field around both their bodies.

"Did you not hear me?" Pryce screamed, clearly displeased with being ignored. "I said 'I win.' You, witch *bitch*."

Defiant, finished with tolerating abuse and slander, Josey gave the witch-hunter an answer—whether he wanted to hear it or not. "What about the statues?" she asked.

Her question stopped his ranting.

Finding him stunned, she pressed forward.

"There are no statues of you. There are statues of Rebecca. There are performances focused on her. We sell children's books and tell the next generation of Fallen Church about her life before they go to bed. There's nothing like that for you."

Sensing a renewed attack, Josey ducked and pushed Nikki flat against the floor. As suspected, Pryce used his powers to lift a table and hurl it across the art room. The table struck the ground and blew apart.

Josey popped back up, confronting the witch-hunter. Now it was her turn to smile. "You're a footnote. Another man who tried to control a woman, only to make her immortal and leave himself a fading memory."

The witch-hunter raised his blunderbuss and pulled the trigger. Again, Josey was ready. Using her powers, she stopped the shot mid-air and sent the pellets back full-force at Pryce. The cloud caught him in the chest, blowing through chunks of thick black clothing and the skin and bone beneath that.

Pryce tossed aside his weapon and shouted for the police officers to open fire. Josey waved her hands, increasing the strength of the protective shielding, pulling it across not only herself and Nikki, but also the injured townspeople scattered across the room.

The witch-hunter drew his cutlass. With his chest a bloody mess, he gave his best war cry and charged at the girls. Josey stood her ground and watched his approach. She knew she had to time everything just right and hoped she'd be able to pull it off.

Arms raised, two-handing the sword as he prepared to bring it down on the supernatural shield, Pryce swung with all his might. In the split second before the blade fell, Josey removed the force-field, catching the witch-hunter by surprise.

His blade fell and Josey's bare hands were there to catch it. The edge of the cutlass dug deep into her flesh, making wounds that would no doubt leave scars. She grunted. But she would not falter, she would *not* be moved.

She whispered harshly. "He's in the circle. The blood is spilled."

Still in shock, Pryce gazed at the damage, taking in the wounds he'd made across his descendant's palms.

But that sight offered him no pleasure, not as he might've hoped for.

Blood oozed from her wounds, like stigmata, running down her arms, down her body, across her pajama pants-covered legs. Then, as though brought to life, the blood moved in swirling funnel cloud-shapes. The brick red, run through with the crackling blue energy, formed a new purple tone as it touched the symbols drawn onto the art room floor, walls, and ceiling.

Watching this, Pryce turned his head, only to find Nikki no longer at Josey's feet, but moved away. During that shocking moment of his initial attack, she'd moved behind the witch-hunter. There, she'd sprinkled salt, replacing what the witch-hunter's boots scuffed away in the attack. There, she read the final words of the spell, the ones written on her arm in black marker—produced the same way that the girls might draw the tattoos they wanted someday, whenever they were bored in class.

Now, Josey smiled. It was a smile she felt damned sure she'd earned. She followed this grin with a primal scream, venting all her anger, frustration, fear, and sadness, pulling from everything that'd held her down, held her back. Following that scream, the witch-hunter's curved blade was flung backward, drawn out of her wound. The blunted edge of the metal caught the man in the face.

Pryce stumbled backward, appearing to teeter on

the edge of disaster. Josey reached for him with bloodied hands, grabbing onto his thick woolen coat.

If he falls out of the circle it's over, she thought.

Luckily, the spell was already working. When she grabbed the front of his coat, she caught a glimpse at his boots where another set of hands, soft and white and shaped almost like hers, reached up from the past —as if time could have a direction other than the usual forward march of progress. The art room floor melted away under her feet, becoming sticks and leaves.

She heard Nikki cry for her from outside the circle. "Josey! Josey, watch out!"

But Josey shook her head, knowing the witch-hunter couldn't be defeated in the present by her alone, the same as how he'd survived in the past when pitted against her ancestor by herself.

This was an old family matter and it would be settled by Josey's family. And Josey's family alone.

And then, she was falling.

CHAPTER TWENTY-THREE

J osey Wesley hit the leaf-strewn floor of the woods outside Fallen Church, a tiny village in the New Hampshire colony. The breath was knocked out of her briefly. Her eyes snapped open, wide. Curled, chilled breaths followed. It took Josey a moment to realize where she was, as though she'd just awakened from a bad dream.

Except what she'd awakened to was far worse than any nightmare. She found herself in the middle of a walking, waking vision of Hell. The bare, skeletal trees, ready for a brutal New England winter, were lit up like matchsticks. Birds and forest creatures scurried amid leaves and twigs and vines, fleeing the roaring flames. The scent of burning pine was on the wind. Mystical energies sizzled and crackled as they were tossed about like grenades. The explosions reminded Josey of the static on her Discman when it was turned up too loud. Looking skyward, she found reds and blues, laced with white-hot lightning, combining into a twisted American flag-like light show.

At the center of this conflagration, her ancestors continued their supernatural combat. The witch Rebecca Wesley and her mentor, paramour, betrayer, and hunter Nathaniel Pryce, were locked in this brutal back-and-forth exchange of unholy, unnatural powers.

Returned to the past, Pryce had found his voice again. A vainglorious, gloating, cocksure voice. His words were laced with venom. Each sharp syllable showcased his rage toward Rebecca. She had defied him, not just in their time, but in the future as well.

"I intended to let *them* kill you," he said. "I was going to give them the honor, the pleasure of it, *witch*. But I see that's not enough. I see now how your message will live on."

He moved toward his former lover, toward the mother of his child.

"So, once I burn you alive, I think I'll go return to the village and wipe Fallen Church off the goddamned maps. Set fire to every man, woman, and child there. Every! One! Just so I can be sure your stain's erased forever."

Josey caught Rebecca faltering, her glowing spectral energy flickering like the flame on Nikki's lighter.

"That's not. . . you can't. . ." Rebecca said, trying to get the words out.

"Can't I?" The witch-hunter's arrogant retort was punctuated by the crackle and pop of more trees burning. "I'm more powerful than you. I always have been. Always will be."

Josey had heard enough. She moved to Rebecca's side. Adding her own powers to those of her ancestor.

"You!" Pryce sneered. "Little girl from a future that will no longer exist. You're hardly as practiced in the dark arts as that witch next to you. Both of your powers pale in comparison to mine."

"You might be more powerful. More skilled. More indebted to dark forces. But you know what else you are?" Josey asked.

She didn't give Pryce a chance to answer.

"You're alone," she said.

With that, she drew the cutlass the witch-hunter had dropped in the future from behind her back and ran full force at the phony Puritan. It was a short distance to Pryce, especially at a sprint. Josey gripped the handle as tight as she could, her blood-slicked hands daubed in dirt and leaf particles. She did her damnedest to ignore the searing pain traveling from her hand and up her arm.

She put her head down, the top of her black hair aimed like an arrow at Pryce's chest. She hoped to feel the impact of her skull cracking against his body, thinking she'd get lucky and crack a rib or two. But before that happened, she felt a sudden squeeze and found her progress halted. She breathed in deeply, inhaling the sweat-soaked odor of the witch-hunter's leather gloves, as he caught her.

Pryce began to mock her. "Foolish girl—"

He didn't get a chance to finish. Because he hadn't

listened to what Josey was saying and had missed her point entirely. But Rebecca?

Rebecca had listened. Rebecca had understood.

As the witch-hunter released her, Josey saw him crashing backward, toppled by Rebecca Wesley launching herself at the man just as her descendant had done. The pair of them, the two women separated by time, but united by blood, climbed on top of the witch-hunter. Punching, tearing, clawing him. Josey took the witch-hunter's sword and stabbed it down into the body of the wicked man. She stabbed as hard as she could and watched the blade cut through cloth and flesh. She did this again and again, over and over.

The attack repeated until the last split second when Josey stopped to study their handiwork. Pryce was not finished and was powering up another spell. His hand, doused in blood, still glowed with his corrupted crimson energy.

"Come on!" Josey shouted to Rebecca.

Both witches grabbed the witch-hunter's arm, pushing it backward, not stopping when he cried out in pain, ignoring the sounds of his bones cracking and tendons tearing. Indeed, they used his bellowing cries to their advantage, taking that blood-slicked gloved hand and shoving it into the witch-hunter's mouth. Pushing as hard as they could, going past his rotted teeth and swollen tongue.

His eyes widened. The energy Pryce had summoned, intending to strike the women, could not be recalled or paused. It could only be released. His cheeks glowed red like a lit Jack-O'-Lantern on Halloween night. The light even penetrated the black of his clothing. Soon, his eyes bulged even more unnaturally from their sockets.

Josey and Rebecca fell back, away from the witch-hunter and onto the smoldering forest floor. Before them, the witch-hunter expanded, bursting at the seams as his wicked magic continued to fill him.

Suddenly, Josey felt a nudge at her arm. Rebecca nodded to the bladed weapon still in her descendant's hands, as if to say, *Go ahead. It's your turn now.*

And Josey was ready to take that turn. She swung the sword like a baseball bat. She swung the curved blade hard, so it struck true and deep, creating a crescent-shaped wound in the witch-hunter's neck.

A spray of crimson, bloody and electric, splashed onto her face, covering her eyes.

As if she'd expended all of her power on that final blow, Josey crumpled to her knees. Somewhere nearby, she heard Rebecca chanting. Lying on her back, Josey stared up from the center of a circle she didn't remember drawing. But there wasn't any sky to be found above her head.

All she saw was Mr. Mundy's classroom ceiling and Nikki's face, tear-streaked, smiling.

Josey reached for that face. She stretched upward, wanting that face more than anything she'd ever wanted.

There would be no more falling. This time, she would fly.

EPILOGUE

Passing through the portal and out the other side, returned to the present, Josey collapsed against Nikki. Still blood-stained, bruised, and sore, Josey was also very much alive. The relief she felt at her continued existence and at her subsequent reunion with the person she cared about more than anything else, made it so she first missed out on all the things around them that differed from the Fallen Church she'd left behind.

Like the fact that they were standing in an open brick-paved pavilion rather than inside the school. Or the fact that Nikki was now dressed in a fancy black gown, pearl buttons clasped up to the neck, with a voluminous skirt hovering like a storm cloud below. All Josey cared about was the fact she was together with the girl she loved.

"Nikki!"

That was all Josey could say, all she *wanted* to say. She gratefully accepted the other girl's embrace, letting her body be pulled in close until their foreheads touched.

Her head tilted, Josey leaned in for a kiss and found the other girl matching her movements as well. Lips parted and they seemed to breathe each other inward until their tongues were dancing, moving nervously at first and then with more surety. It was as magical a first kiss as Josey could've hoped for.

When they finally stopped, Josey laughed, overwhelmed by the emotions racing inside, each of them vying for prominence.

"That was... that was... incredible."

"I'm glad to hear it, Goodwitch Josephine," Nikki said.

"But you never call me Josephi..."

Josey trailed off as she finally noticed the glow of mystical energy in her friend's eyes. She tilted her head up and back, taking in the blue-tinted, sun-dappled early morning sky of Fallen Church. The pale expanse was crowded with witches, young and old, men and women, all of them flying. Soaring through the open air, free and fearless.

Taking in these impossible sights, Josey wondered just where or *when* she'd traveled to. To a different time, a different world, one where Nathaniel Pryce had died and Rebecca Wesley had lived. The realization of what that change meant, of how far-reaching its consequences might have been slowly sank in for Josey.

The night of the witch-hunter had ended, but the witches' day had just begun.

STOP ■

ACKNOWLEDGMENTS

Unlike many other books of arcane knowledge and terrible secrets, this particular tome was not written, crafted, and published in solitude. And thank goodness for that! I'd like to take a moment to pay tribute to the many who added their own bits of magic to the mix.

First, thanks to Alan Lastufka for being open to the pitch and for taking on this witch-tacular project. Your editorial insights helped elevate the story to the next level and you are a true pro through and through. One of the absolute best publishers to work with and I'm so grateful for this collaboration and others ahead. I can't imagine a better home for Night of the Witch-Hunter than the Killer VHS line at Shortwave.

Thanks also to other key team member who've helped make this book as wickedly good as it can possibly be. Line editor Nancy LaFever and proofreader Erin Foster demonstrate the vital importance of getting one's magic words in just the right order.

Thanks to their efforts, this story became the book in your hands and not—I dunno—a frog.

And Marc Vuletich (aka Vulture34) conjured up cover art that perfectly captures the mood and overall vibe of the tale being told. From front to back, this book is wrapped up in so goddamn beautiful artwork, and I wouldn't have it any other way.

Finally, and forever, thanks to my family. Jenna, Grant, and Avery, thank you for your patience, your inspiration, and the constant swirling chaos that we dance amid every single day.

ABOUT THE AUTHOR

Patrick Barb is an author of weird, dark, and horrifying tales, currently living (and trying not to freeze to death) in Saint Paul, Minnesota. His published works include the dark fiction collections *The Children's Horror* and *Pre-Approved for Haunting,* the novellas *Gargantuana's Ghost, Turn,* and *JK-LOL,* as well as the novelette *Helicopter Parenting in the Age of Drone Warfare.*

He is the editor and publisher of the anthology *And One Day We Will Die: Strange Stories Inspired by the Music of Neutral Milk Hotel.* His forthcoming works include his talking animal/ crime/cosmic horror novella *The Nut House* from Undertaker Books and his debut sci-fi/horror novel *Abducted* from Dark Matter Ink. His interview column "Your Favorite Author's Favorite Author" is a monthly feature in Shortwave Magazine. Finally, his 2023 short story "The Scare Groom" was selected for *Best Horror of the Year Volume 16.*

Visit him at patrickbarb.com.

A NOTE FROM SHORTWAVE

Thank you for reading the sixth Killer VHS Series book! If you enjoyed *Night of the Witch-Hunter*, please consider writing a review. Reviews help readers find more titles they may enjoy, and that helps us continue to publish titles like this.

For more Shortwave titles, visit us online...

OUR WEBSITE

shortwavepublishing.com

SOCIAL MEDIA

@ShortwaveBooks

EMAIL US

contact@shortwavepublishing.com